INVITATION ONLY
MURDER

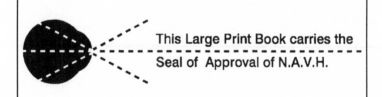

This Large Print Book carries the
Seal of Approval of N.A.V.H.

A LUCY STONE MYSTERY

INVITATION ONLY MURDER

LESLIE MEIER

THORNDIKE PRESS
A part of Gale, a Cengage Company

**LIBRARY OF CONGRESS CIP DATA ON FILE.
CATALOGUING IN PUBLICATION FOR THIS BOOK
IS AVAILABLE FROM THE LIBRARY OF CONGRESS**

ISBN-13: 978-1-4328-7170-3 (hardcover alk. paper)

Published in 2019 by arrangement with Kensington Books, an imprint
of Kensington Publishing Corp.

Printed in Mexico
1 2 3 4 5 6 7 23 22 21 20 19

For Mary Littleford and
John C. Littleford,
who introduced me to the island

CHAPTER ONE

The little bell on the door to the *Pennysaver* newspaper office in the quaint coastal town of Tinker's Cove, Maine, jangled and Lucy Stone looked up from the story she was writing about the new recycling regulations — paper, glass, and plastic would not be accepted unless clean and separate, no more single stream — to see who had come in, and smiled broadly. It was her oldest and best friend, Sue Finch, looking every bit as stylish and put-together as usual with her dark hair cut in a neat bob and dressed in her usual summer uniform: striped French fisherman's jersey, black Bermudas, espadrilles, and straw sun hat. Skipping a greeting, Sue pulled an envelope from her straw carryall with a perfectly manicured hand and declared, "Guess what came in today's mail? It's an invitation to die for!"

Lucy, who was used to playing second fiddle to Sue, raised an inquisitive eyebrow.

She was also dressed in her usual summer uniform: a freebie T-shirt from the lumberyard, a pair of cutoff jeans, and neon orange running shoes. She hadn't bothered to style her hair this sunny June morning, thinking that it looked fine, and had missed a stubborn lock in back that curled up like a drake's tail feather. "Do tell," she said, leaning back in her desk chair.

"Just look at the paper," cooed Sue, pulling a square of sturdy card out of the velvet-smooth lined envelope. "Handmade. And the lettering is hand-pressed. And, oh, the address on the envelope was done by a calligrapher," she continued, handing the envelope to Lucy. "Trust me, something like this doesn't come cheap."

"Is it a wedding invitation?" asked Lucy, admiring the elaborate, swirling script on the front of the envelope. Turning the envelope over and studying the back, she recognized the formally identified senders: Mr. and Mrs. Scott Newman. Everybody in town had heard of the Newmans, who had recently bought an island off the coast and proceeded to hire every contractor in the county to restore the property's long-abandoned buildings, including spending a fortune to save the magnificent barn that was considered an architectural master-piece.

"No, it's for a 'night to remember,' that's what they're calling it," replied Sue, handing Lucy the invitation. "It's to celebrate the Newman family's donation of the island to the Coastal Maine Land Trust and to thank all the people who worked on the restoration."

"I bet we're invited, too, then," said Lucy, whose husband, Bill, a restoration carpenter, had been the lead contractor for the project. "The invitation's probably in the mailbox at home."

"It's going to be fabulous, if this invitation is any indication," said Sue. "No expense spared and believe me, the Newmans have plenty of expense to spare."

Lucy knew all about Scott Newman; she'd written a profile of the billionaire venture capitalist when rumors started floating that he was interested in acquiring Fletcher's Island for his family's summer vacations. When she interviewed him, she'd been somewhat surprised to learn that he was a keen preservationist who was interested in keeping the island completely off the grid and was refusing to install modern innovations, allowing only the original nineteenth-century technology. He planned to collect rainwater in a cistern, use a primitive electric generation system, and cook on an enormous woodstove, all of which were considered wonderfully advanced when the island was developed by lumber tycoon Edward T. Fletcher. When Lucy asked if this wasn't rather impractical, Newman had replied that it was modern life that was impractical, citing scientific studies linking climate change to human activity. "The old ways were much kinder to the environment, and face it, we've only got one planet, there's no planet B," he declared. "We've got to take care of Earth, or we're all doomed."

Some of the locals hired to work on the restoration project had a good laugh over Newman's proclaimed environmental stewardship, as restoring the nineteenth-century structures required using thousands of kilowatts of eletricity, provided by gas-greedy portable generators. His insistence on using authentic materials such as lath and horsehair plaster rather than Sheetrock, and searching out recycled flooring, windows, and doors, not to mention hardware, had required lots of workers who had to be ferried to and from the island on power boats that burned gallons of fossil fuel. "It's like the cloth versus disposable diapers thing," Bill had told her. "Sure, the disposables fill up the landfill, but washing the cloth diapers uses water and energy. It's kind of six of one and half a dozen of the other when it comes to the environment."

Most controversial was the restoration of the immense barn, which alone was estimated to cost at least two million dollars. The huge number of cedar shingles required for the roof and siding had created an industry shortage that sent the price skyrocketing and shook the commodities market. The *Pennysaver* had received numerous letters to the editor protesting the shingle shortage and arguing that there were better ways to spend so much money. One writer proposed restoring the sprawling local elementary school, for example, which he claimed was a prime example of 1960s architecture.

Locals had also refused to be bamboozled by Newman's supposed generosity in donating the island to the land trust, while reserving his right to retain it for his own use during his lifetime. It was true that he'd also preserved the rights of the Hopkins family, long-term residents of the island, to remain there, but again, only during his lifetime. And while the agreement set limits on how the island could be used, and was intended to preserve the island's environment in perpetuity, the gift had come with plenty of strings attached and had garnered a large tax deduction for the Newmans, a fact that many writers of letters to the editor had also pointed out.

Despite the controversy, however, the party was eagerly anticipated by everyone who received an invitation, and that included land trust board members, contractors, local officials, and media, which was pretty much a who's who of the entire town. The question that was on everyone's lips as the big day drew closer was, how were the Newmans going to pull off such a big party while preserving their nineteenth-century lifestyle? Sue Finch wasn't the only one to wonder, "Are we going to have to swim there? And are we all going to be sitting in the dark, huddled around a campfire, toasting wienies on sticks?"

Lucy was pondering that very question when she drove home from work a week or so later and found a rusting and dented old Subaru parked in her driveway. The car was missing a couple of hubcaps, had a crumpled front fender, and the glass on a rear window had been replaced with duct tape and a plastic grocery bag. Continuing her examination with the keen eye of an investigative reporter, she noticed the registration tag was out of date, and so was the required state inspection sticker.

Climbing the porch steps of the antique farmhouse that she and Bill had renovated and entering the kitchen, she was greeted by her aging black Lab, Libby. Arthritis didn't stop Libby from rising stiffly from her comfy dog bed and wagging her tail in welcome, earning her a treat and a pat on the head from Lucy.

Voices could be heard in the adjacent family room and Lucy stuck her head in, curious to learn who owned the Subaru. "Oh, hi, Mom," said her daughter Zoe, quickly disentangling herself from the arms of a shabby-looking fellow with a stubbly, three-day beard. "Mom, this is Mike Snider."

Mike didn't bother to get up from the comfy sectional where he was reclining, or even to lift his head from the throw pillow it was resting on. "Hiya," he said, raising one hand and giving a little flap.

Lucy glared at him, taking in his shaved head, tattooed neck, and torn jeans that clearly needed a wash. Worst of all was the T-shirt with a message that was clearly unprintable for a family newspaper like the *Pennysaver*. "Hiya, yourself," said Lucy,

13

turning on her heel and marching out of the room, leaving no doubt that this was a situation that did not meet with her approval.

Back in the kitchen, Lucy got busy on dinner, noisily pulling pots out of cabinets and slamming them down on the stove. She was filling a pasta pot with water when the couple appeared, holding hands, and were met with a low growl from Libby, who watched Mike through narrowed eyes and flattened ears from her doggy bed. She was clearly considering getting to her feet, painful though it would be, when Mike reached for the knob and pulled the door open. "Catch ya later," he said, before stepping through the doorway. Moments later, Lucy heard the roar of the Subaru's unmuffled engine, which sputtered out a few times before catching and carrying Mike away.

"Who is he? And where did you meet him?" Lucy demanded, turning to face Zoe. Zoe was her youngest, and every bit as pretty as her older sisters, Elizabeth and Sara. She shared Elizabeth's dark hair and petite build, but had Sara's peachy skin and pouty lips. Today she was glowing, no doubt the result of her aborted activities on the sectional.

"At school, Mom," she answered, referring to Winchester College, a local liberal arts university where she was a junior, currently majoring in French after trying political science, psychology, and art history. She had hopes of joining Elizabeth in Paris, where her older sister was working as an assistant concierge at the toney Cavendish Hotel. "Mike's a TA in the computer science department. He's really smart. Even Sara says so," she added, bolstering her case with a reference to the family's doubting Thomas, who was a grad student at Winchester.

"He might be smart," admitted Lucy, "but he's certainly not socialized. Libby has better manners, and she's a dog."

"He's a little rough around the edges," said Zoe, beaming, "but Libby only gets up to greet you because she knows you'll give her a treat."

"That was unkind," retorted Lucy, bending over the dog and scratching her behind her ears. "You love me, you really, really love me, don't you?"

The dog yawned and settled her chin on her front paws.

"And that car," said Lucy, reverting to the subject at hand. "The registration's lapsed and so has the inspection, which is understandable since I doubt it would pass. It definitely needs a new muffler."

"Mike's got better things to think about than bother with stuff like that. He's working on a computer game that's going to be revolutionary, that's going to change everything."

"Well, if you ask me, he'd be better off taking a shower and changing into clean clothes."

"Oh, you don't understand anything!" declared Zoe, storming up the stairs to her room, where she slammed the door.

"What was that all about?" asked Bill, stepping into the kitchen and kissing his wife on the cheek, before depositing his empty lunch cooler on the counter. Lucy smiled, noticing that Libby didn't get up for him, but did manage to thump her tail a few times.

"Zoe's got a new boyfriend," explained Lucy. "A real loser."

"She'll learn," said Bill, opening the refrigerator door and extracting a can of beer. "She's got to figure these things out for herself."

"Just you wait until you meet him," said Lucy, tearing up lettuce for salad. "I bet you'll change your tune then."

Bill sat down at the round, golden oak table and popped the tab on his beer.

"Whaddya think about this island shindig?" he asked, with a nod at the invitation that was stuck to the refrigerator door with a retro magnet advertising Moxie soda pop. "I'm not gonna have to wear a jacket and tie, am I?"

"No jackets, no ties," said Lucy, repeating the verdict Sue had handed down when Lucy called for advice. "It's resort casual."

So Bill was togged out in a navy polo, Nantucket red shorts, and boat shoes, and Lucy was wearing de rigueur white jeans, embroidered tunic, and sandals when they joined the assembled guests at the appointed day and hour at the harbor in Tinker's Cove. It was a balmy evening, but these Mainers weren't fooled by the thermometer and were carrying windbreakers for the breezy boat ride.

"How are they getting us out there?" wondered Ted Stillings, Lucy's boss at the *Pennysaver.* "Newman is a big fan of sail."

"Yeah, he's got a beautiful restored yacht, a cutter," added Sid Finch, Sue's husband, with a hint of envy in his voice. "But it's not gonna hold all these people."

The dock was indeed crowded. It seemed as if most of the town had been invited, and spirits were high with anticipation. They

17

were all expecting the promised night to remember, but weren't sure exactly what that might be. When two of the puffin watch boats that carried sightseers out to view the colorful birds that were the Maine version of penguins hove into view and chugged up to the dock, there was a heightened sense of excitement.

"Well, we're off!" sang Sue, as they settled themselves on wooden benches for the ten-mile crossing to the island.

Ninety minutes later, the boats had crossed the ten miles between town and the Fletcher's Island dock, where Scott Newman and his wife awaited them. Lily Starr was Scott's second, much younger wife, and before her marriage had a rising career as a country-western singer. Even in flats she was slightly taller than Scott, who was a slight man with very short, very dark hair who seemed barely able to contain his intense energy. "I trust you had a pleasant crossing," he said, as the gangplank was lowered and the guests began to debark from the boat. "Welcome to Fletcher's Island."

The couple stood together by the gangplank, taking each guest by the hand and helping them negotiate the steep incline, welcoming them, and instructing them to

18

follow the illuminated path that led from the landing up to the barn. Dusk was falling and Lucy was grateful for the lighted luminarias, most probably constructed of biodegradable paper bags and soy candles, that lit the way along the gravel road that gradually ascended to the island's summit. As they rounded a bend, the massive, newly restored barn came into view, causing people to catch their breath at the amazing sight. Light glowed in the many windows of the huge structure, which had a unique sloping roof topped by five illuminated cupolas and two soaring silos at either end topped with conical roofs. The barn was surrounded by a cluster of outbuildings, including an icehouse, creamery, henhouse, as well as the modest stone house occupied by the Hopkins family. The Fletcher mansion, which had also been restored and was now the Newmans' summer home, was on the south end of the island, some distance from the barn, and the party.

Continuing along the road that circled the barn and outbuildings, Lucy entered the barnyard, where she joined the other guests, who were oohing and aahing over the spectacular view and the gorgeous sunset.

"Not too shabby," said Sue in an approving tone of voice, taking in the expanse of rosy sky and silvery ocean dotted with small, pine-covered islands.

"And the barn, just look at it," said Lucy, sighing. The roof alone was sixty feet at its highest point, and the thought of the slippery slope the roofers had to negotiate gave her the shivers. The huge doors stood open invitingly, so they went into the large space that was illuminated by old-fashioned lanterns. Enormous arrangements of daisies, grasses, and meadow flowers decorated tables covered with blue-and-white checked cloths, and bales of hay topped with matching checked pillows offered plenty of seating. "Is that a bar?" asked Bill, interrupting her thoughts.

"I believe so," said Sid, and the two men strode off purposefully, followed by their wives.

The bartender was a remarkably good-looking young man with blond hair and a neatly trimmed beard, wearing a black T-shirt printed with a map of the island and the words QUAHOG REPUBLIC. A name badge announced his name was Wolfgang, and a slight German accent indicated he wasn't a local.

"Are you working here for the summer?" inquired Lucy, aware that the plentiful summer jobs in Maine attracted college students from all over the world.

"I'm from Berlin," he said. "I was hoping to work in one of the craft breweries. I heard there are a lot of them in Maine, but this came up and I like it here." He nodded, looking around at the island in approval. "What can I get you?"

The two couples had no sooner been supplied with drinks, beer for the men and white wine for the women, when they were approached by two attractive young women offering trays of hors d'oeuvres: tiny crab cakes, chicken wings, and deviled eggs. "I'm Parker, and I just want to let you know there's cheese and crackers and crudités on the table over there," said the first, who appeared to be in her late twenties and was dressed in a bright pink Lilly Pulitzer–style shift and bare feet.

"And I'm Taylor," said the second server, who appeared to be an identical twin of the first, dressed in a blue and green Lilly Pulitzer and bare feet, adding, "and there's a raw bar next to it."

"Thank you," said Lucy, taking one of the crab cakes. "Are you girls going to be here all summer?"

"We sure are," said Taylor. "Dad's really keen on having the whole family together for this first summer on the island. He's put

21

us to work monitoring a puffin colony on the back side of the island."

"That must be really interesting," said Lucy, who had realized the girls must be Scott Newman's daughters, probably from his first marriage.

"And important work," added Sue, surprising Lucy by taking one of the proffered crab cakes. Sue rarely ate anything that could be classified as actual food, and seemed to exist on a diet of black coffee and white wine.

"You should try the deviled eggs, they're from our own chickens," said Parker.

"And the wings?" asked Lucy, with a mischievous smile.

"I'm not sure about those," said Taylor, with a little smile. "But Dad does want the island to become self-sufficient. We're starting with the chickens and goats, and there's a big vegetable garden, too."

"Don't miss the raw bar; it's over by the milking parlor," added Parker as she too drifted off, carrying their offerings to the other guests.

"What cute girls," said Lucy. "Fancy a bit of cheese?"

"Are you out of your mind?" snorted Sue. "Cheese is full of fat and calories, while oysters, on the other hand, are nothing but sea water and lean protein."

"Oysters it is, then," said Lucy, as the two made their way to the raw bar, where their husbands were already working on second helpings. Another good-looking fellow, this one dark-haired and brown-skinned, was shucking oysters, and Lucy wondered if an attractive appearance was a requirement for working on the island. The shucker was also wearing a Quahog Republic T-shirt, and his name badge gave his name as Ben.

"Are you also a foreign student, like Wolf?" asked Lucy, plucking an oyster from its bed of ice.

"Not unless you think Brooklyn is a foreign country," he replied, smiling and revealing very white teeth.

"It almost is, to us Mainers," said Sue, nibbling on a huge shrimp. "I suppose you wanted to get out of the city and get some fresh Maine air?" Sue's daughter, Sidra, lived in Brooklyn, and Sue was forever complaining about the air, which she said smelled of diesel exhaust from the buses.

"Yup," replied Ben, cocking an eyebrow and adopting a bit of an attitude. "I'm just a big Fresh Air kid, straight off the bus."

"I think you mean straight off the boat," said Lucy, trying one of the shrimp. While chewing she noticed a distinct chill in Ben's attitude, and was quick to make amends. "I really didn't mean that the way it sounded. All I meant was that you can't take a bus to an island."

"Don't miss the clambake," advised Ben, with a rather curt nod toward a column of smoke that was rising outside on a grassy area behind the barn. "It ought to be just about ready."

"Thanks for the advice," said Lucy, grabbing Sue's hand and looking for their husbands, who had wandered off in the direction of the bar. "We've got to get the guys; they won't want to miss it."

Word had quickly spread among the guests, who were streaming toward the clambake, which was just being uncovered by two young men also wearing the black T-shirts. Lucy recognized them as Will and Brad Hopkins, lobstermen she'd often seen unloading their catch at the lobster pound in Tinker's Cove. The two were taking instruction from an older man she suspected was their grandfather, Hopp Hopkins. She'd never met him, but had heard of him, as the legendary paterfamilias of the Hopkins clan. The family had stubbornly remained on the island after other members of a once-thriving fishing community had sought greener pastures elsewhere, and Lucy won-

24

dered what the Hopkinses really thought of Scott Newman and his family. Were they pleased to work for the billionaire, or did they resent taking orders from a newcomer? Whichever it was, the Hopkins men were too busy to think about it, raking off the smoking seaweed and fishing out steaming net bags containing the traditional clams, lobster, corn, and potatoes. Soon everyone was seated at long outdoor tables covered with checked cloths and lit with glowing oil lamps, cracking open their lobsters and clams, and dipping the meat into melted butter. The wine and beer flowed, and the atmosphere was lively and friendly, since nothing breaks down social barriers like the messy process of eating lobster in the rough.

The lobster was followed by dessert, a choice of strawberry shortcake or hand-churned goat's milk ice cream, both made by Susan Hopkins. Susan, Hopp's daughter-in-law and Will and Brad's mother, was rarely seen in Tinker's Cove, but did come to town a couple of times a year to see the dentist or shop for supplies. Lucy had tried to catch her on one of those visits to interview her about her island life, but Susan had demurred. "I've really nothing to say," she'd said, "and I do have to get back home." She'd then glanced anxiously toward the harbor, where Hopp was waiting for her in the family's lobster boat, and Lucy had wondered if Susan was a victim of domestic abuse. Tonight, however, she seemed at ease in her black apron with the white Quahog Republic logo, smiling as she doled out the delicious desserts.

People were just finishing up the last of their cake and ice cream when music could be heard. "A live band?" wondered Lucy aloud, as they tossed their biodegradable paper plates and bamboo forks into the trash and headed toward the dance floor, lured by the sound of a bluegrass band. The dance floor was located in the former hayloft, which was reached by climbing a flight of stairs that had been cleverly constructed in one of the silos.

"I know you want to work off some of that dinner by dancing," said Scott Newman, speaking to the gathered guests. "But first we have some official business to take care of." He then introduced the board members of the Maine Coast Land Trust, including Roger Wilcox, the board president. Wilcox then took over, producing a deed for the transfer of the island to the trust, which both he and Scott signed with great ceremony. The men shook hands, and Lucy used her phone to take a grin-and-grab

26

photo for the *Pennysaver;* then everyone settled in for the obligatory speeches.

Wilcox was brief, saying the addition of Fletcher's Island to the trust's other properties was a significant step in preserving Maine's unique history and island ecology, and would provide an important habitat for local wildlife such as seals and the threatened population of puffins. He then turned the mike over to Jonathan Franke, the trust's chief executive. Lucy remembered him as the long-haired and Birkenstocked environmental agitator who had been instrumental in creating the Association for the Preservation of Tinker's Cove. That organization of earnest citizens had continued to maintain the town's conservation area, but without Franke. He had now cut his hair and shaved his beard, and was dressed in business casual befitting his new role with the trust.

"I'll be brief," promised Franke, "but I do want to say how grateful we at the trust are to be the beneficiaries of Scott Newman's incredible generosity. It's thanks to his foresight and his commitment to the environment that Fletcher's Island will become a natural preserve, providing habitat for a large variety of seabirds, including the threatened Atlantic puffins. I know there has been some controversy about the nature of the gift, and I want to assure everyone that Scott Newman himself was insistent that the island eventually be restored as closely as possible to a natural condition. The buildings, including this magnificent historical barn, will remain and will be used for educational and research purposes. So, in closing, on behalf of all the members and officers of the trust, I want to express once again our gratitude and appreciation to Scott Newman."

Led by Franke, the gathered company joined in giving Scott an enthusiastic round of applause as he took the microphone and held up his hand in a modest protest at the applause.

"Thank you so much," he said, again signaling that the applause should end. "As I'm sure you all know, the donation of the island was only possible because of the success of my company, New World Capital. We venture capitalists often get a bum rap, and I admit we must accept our fair share of blame for putting money ahead of environmental concerns, but I am happy to say that we at New World are taking a different tack, and our success has been built by investing in environmentally conscious and beneficial technologies. The experts, the economists, and the guys at Wharton and other top business schools said it couldn't be done, but we proved them wrong. New World Capital has done very well, you could even say exceptionally well, by committing to following tough environmental standards, and I attribute a good portion of that success to my daughter, Parker. It was Parker who came home from kindergarten one day and asked, 'Dad, what are you doing for the environment?' At that time, I simply didn't have an answer, but I looked at my little girl and promised myself that I was going to do everything I could to preserve her future and the future of millions of other little children like her. That's how New World Capital came to be and tonight, on this very special occasion, I'm happy to announce that Parker Newman will become a full partner in the company." He signaled to his daughter to join him and she did, bowing her head bashfully as everyone applauded.

This news struck Lucy as surprising, since she had rather patronizingly, she now realized, considered Parker a pampered, overprivileged rich girl who was doing a nice job serving hors d'oeuvres.

After the polite applause died down, Newman went on to praise his other daughter, Taylor. "She's an absolute PR whiz, and you can all thank her for this fabulous party — it was her idea."

The appreciative guests' applause was somewhat more enthusiastic for Taylor, who encouraged everyone to stay and dance to the music. The band took the cue and struck up a lively tune, prompting a few brave souls to take to the dance floor. Bill and Sid headed over to the bar, which had been moved to the loft, and Lucy decided she really ought to check with Taylor, making sure she had her facts straight for the story she would write about the party and the transfer to the land trust.

Taylor was standing with her father when Lucy approached and introduced herself. The pair greeted her warmly, asking how they could help. "I just need to check some facts, make sure I've got everybody's name spelled right," said Lucy.

"Of course. I've prepared a press packet," said Taylor. "It's downstairs in the office. I'll be back in a minute."

Taylor dashed off, leaving Lucy standing rather awkwardly with Scott Newman. "This is quite a party," she said, breaking the ice.

"I'm glad you're enjoying it," said Scott.

"I'd love to interview you sometime about your lifestyle choice here," said Lucy. "I know you're very interested in environmental stewardship and historical preservation."

Newman was thoughtful, gazing off in the distance. "That's a good idea. Why don't you come and stay here with us on the island for a few days? Then you'd get to see what we're doing firsthand. How about it?"

"That would be great," said Lucy, as Taylor trotted toward them, a folder in her hand. "I'd have to check with my editor, of course. How can I get back to you?" Lucy was aware that the island was off the grid, and presumably that meant no cell phone service.

"Taylor will get in touch with you . . ." he said, turning around rather abruptly and greeting another guest.

"Don't mind Dad, he's always thinking," said Taylor, returning and presenting her with the folder.

Lucy smiled and took the folder. "This will be very helpful. I probably ought to mention that he invited me to the island so I could experience the lifestyle and write about it in more depth for the paper."

Taylor's eyebrow rose in surprise. "Did he, now?" She smiled warmly. "I guess that means I'll have to work out the details and get in touch with you."

"I'll be looking forward to hearing from

you," said Lucy, fingering the folder.

"Great." Taylor nodded, dismissing her. "Don't miss the music," she urged. "It's the Brian Brown Blues Band," she said, naming a group Lucy vaguely remembered from her college days. "And Lily's promised to sing."

This really is a night to remember, thought Lucy, turning and looking for Bill. She spotted him standing on the edge of the dance floor, holding a beer, and joined him, taking his hand. The song was ending and Lily took the stage, dressed in a flowery, diaphanous dress with many fluttering layers, and stood behind the mike. She began to sing a sad song about love lost, and Bill slipped his arm around Lucy's waist. They stood together, swaying slightly to the music, and Lucy thought nothing could be more perfect than that moment. Not ever.

CHAPTER TWO

When Lucy awoke on Sunday morning, she wasn't sure if last night on the island had really happened or if it was a dream. When she went downstairs to the kitchen, where Bill was humming the tune from the band's last dance while sautéing vegetables for a Spanish omelet, she knew it wasn't a dream at all.

"That really was a wonderful night," she said, slipping her arms around his waist and hugging him.

Bill turned, spatula in hand, and kissed her. "I remember everything, including you in some pretty compromising positions," he said with a leer.

True enough, the romantic atmosphere had continued after their moonlit return home on the puffin boat, when the couple had tiptoed upstairs, stifling giggles, so as not to wake their sleeping daughters. They had tried to be quiet while making love, but

Lucy feared a squeaky bedspring might have given them away.

"Shhh," she said, hushing him and pointing upstairs. "The girls might hear you."

"Lucy, Sara and Zoe aren't children anymore. I'm pretty sure they know they weren't found under cabbage leaves in the garden."

"Well, we don't need to flaunt it," said Lucy, as a noisy motor was heard outside. She slipped out of her husband's arms and went to look out the window, where she saw Mike Snider's wreck of a Subaru idling noisily in the driveway. The passenger door opened and Zoe stepped out, tossing a kiss to Mike as he revved the engine and drove off. Then she bounded up the porch steps and into the kitchen.

Lucy's jaw dropped. All this time she'd assumed that Zoe was asleep in her bed, but she wasn't there at all. She'd been out all night with Mike Snider.

"What's going on?" she demanded, when the door flew open and Zoe breezed in.

"Oh, Mom. Dad." Zoe looked uneasy. "I thought you'd be at church."

"We had a late night and decided to sleep in," said Bill, looking rather stern.

"So you thought you could sneak in the house after spending the night with . . . with that . . ." Lucy struggled to find the right word, finally finishing her question by adding, "With that creep?"

Zoe was quick with a response. "Nothing like that. It's just I had a couple of beers and didn't want to drive."

"Drive?" Bill was on it in a flash. "You didn't take your car. It's still in the driveway."

It was true. Zoe's little silver Corolla was parked in its usual spot.

Sensing defeat, Zoe went on the offensive. "Gee, you guys are so suspicious. Don't you trust me?"

"It's not you I don't trust. It's Mike."

"Well," said Zoe, aiming to regain some dignity, "you have nothing to fear. Mike is a perfect gentleman." She added a little sniff for emphasis. "And I'm over twenty-one and my private life is none of your business." And with that she swept out of the room and up the stairs.

"She has a point," said Bill, flipping the finished omelet on a plate and setting it on the table.

"Believe me, nothing good is going to come of this," said Lucy, dividing the omelet in halves. "She could get pregnant."

"I've got a shotgun, if it comes to that," said Bill, pouring coffee.

"Don't even joke about it," said Lucy, already playing out several scenarios in her mind: Zoe dropping out of school, Zoe working two jobs to support Mike, Zoe pregnant and destitute, Zoe abandoned and heartbroken.

"Eat up," urged Bill, noticing that Lucy hadn't touched her breakfast.

"I've kind of lost my appetite," said Lucy, scooping her eggs into Libby's bowl, where they were eagerly scarfed up by the dog. Libby never lost her appetite and wagged her tail by way of a thank-you for the morning treat.

Zoe's relationship with Mike Snider had only grown more intense as the weeks passed and Lucy prepared to return to the island. Taylor had been good as her word, promptly following up on the offered invitation, suggesting that Lucy come for the Fourth of July holiday, when the whole Newman family would be gathered on Fletcher's Island.

"That way you'll get a feeling for what life on the island is all about and what Dad has accomplished," she'd said, speaking with Lucy on the phone. "It's really pretty amazing, and I think you'll be impressed."

So, Lucy was waiting on the dock at the

appointed time with a duffel packed with warm clothes and plenty of sunscreen, battery-powered tape recorder and flash-light, as well as extra batteries. She felt a bit like a kid going off to summer camp, which was a big relief from the tension at home. Zoe had continued to see Mike, despite the disapproval of her parents and even her older sister, Sara. She was rarely home, skip-ping family meals and instead rooting in the refrigerator for leftovers at odd hours, and was uncommunicative during her rare ap-pearances, constantly staring at her phone. Lucy and Bill had a running argument about Zoe, with Lucy insisting they do something, although not sure what, while Bill thought it was best to let Zoe work things out for herself. Sara, for her part, seethed with resentment, jealous that Zoe had a boyfriend when she didn't and angry about the upset the relationship was caus-ing at home. It was no wonder, thought Lucy, that she was looking forward to get-ting away for a while to enjoy some peace and quiet.

"Welcome to the nineteenth century," yelled Ben, as Wolf steered a chubby catboat up to the dock. It was a neat bit of seaman-ship, since the boat was powered only by sail and was heavily laden with provisions.

"Come on board," urged Ben, seizing her duffel and adding it to the piled-up boxes and waterproof totes. "There's plenty of room," he added, clearing off a space for her to sit on a plastic crate.

"Coming about," sang out Wolf, and Lucy obediently ducked her head as the boom swung around and the sail caught the wind. Then they were off, zipping across the harbor at a good clip, thanks to a brisk breeze.

It was a beautiful day for a sail, sunny and warm, with just enough wind to speed the catboat, but not so much that the sea became choppy. As they flew along, Lucy realized how quiet it was with no engine noise. Conversation was possible, so she got right to work, pulling her reporter's notebook out of her duffel.

"For the record, I want you to know that I'm a reporter, working on a story about the island. For starters, I need your full names and ages. Okay?"

"Sure," said Ben. "I'm Benicio Martinez, and I'm twenty-two."

"And I'm Wolfgang Drucker, twenty-five."

"So, how do you guys like living and working on the island?"

"It's okay," said Ben, who was seated in the rear of the boat, manning the tiller.

"There's plenty of good food, comfortable beds . . ."

"Cold water showers," said Wolf, with a shudder.

"That's good, 'cause there's no girls," offered Ben, with a twinkle in his eye.

"No available girls, you mean," teased Wolf.

"It's a summer job." Ben shrugged. "We get plenty of fresh air and exercise, every day's a little bit different. It's okay."

"What about cell phones?" inquired Lucy, who knew that her daughters were rarely parted from their devices.

"Not allowed," said Wolf, "but it doesn't matter because the reception is lousy, anyway."

Lucy was skeptical. "And you don't mind living like it's 1850?"

"It's not bad, really," said Ben. "You'll be surprised."

"Yeah, you kind of get into it," agreed Wolf, growing philosophical. "It makes you think about all the rest. Modern life, no? Facebook and everything comes at you so fast. Slow is better, I think."

"What's with the Quahog Republic T-shirts?" asked Lucy, curious about the shirts that seemed to be an island uniform.

"A joke, I think," said Wolf.

39

"Scott's idea," said Ben, with a smirk. "It's like the island is his own little country."

"What about the Hopkinses? Are they happy with this new arrangement?" asked Lucy, hoping they wouldn't think she was a nosy parker.

Ben and Wolf shared a glance; then they encountered a bit of chop from a passing speedboat and had to turn their attention to keeping the overloaded boat upright. "I swear they do that on purpose," snorted Wolf, giving the already-distant cigarette boat an evil eye.

The two men didn't pick up the conversation, and Lucy felt the moment for confidences had passed, so she sat quietly, enjoying the experience of spending a morning afloat. Even though Tinker's Cove was a coastal town, where boats outnumbered cars, Lucy and Bill had remained landlubbers. With four kids to feed and educate, and an old house to maintain, there'd never been any extra money for a boat larger than a canoe. Bill had always joked that it was better to have friends with boats than to own a boat, and Lucy thought there was some truth to that. Nevertheless, she loved boating and eagerly accepted any invitation that came her way for a sail.

Too soon, it seemed to her, the island hove

into sight and then they were docking, greeted by Brad Hopkins, who cheerfully got to work unloading the boat. The three young men were busy sorting out the supplies, so Lucy picked up her duffel and started climbing the path up the hill to the barn. When she reached the barnyard, she encountered Newman's twin boys, Walter and Fred, who were wearing superhero capes and were chasing each other on the grassy lawn where the clambake was held.

"Superman's stronger," yelled one.

"No, Iron Man is strongest," countered the other.

Watching them, Lucy smiled, thinking of her grandson, Patrick, who lived far away in Alaska with his parents, her son, Toby, and his wife, Molly. Suddenly, one of the boys noticed her and stopped abruptly. "Who are you?" he demanded.

"I'm Lucy. Who are you?"

"I'm Fred," he replied, and Lucy studied the two identical twins closely, looking for some distinguishing feature. She didn't want to spend her entire stay calling the boys by the wrong names.

"I'm Walter," said the other, and Lucy noticed he was slightly heavier, with a rounder face.

"Well, I'm glad to meet you. I'm here to

visit with your parents. Do you know where they are?"

"Mom's in the garden," said Fred, who seemed to be the more dominant twin. "Wanna see her?"

"We can show you the goats on the way," offered Walter.

"Goats! That would be great." She paused, conscious of her heavy duffel. "I've got this bag . . ."

"Just put it down. Someone will take care of it," said Fred, with the nonchalance of a child lucky enough to be born to wealthy parents. The Newmans clearly had people who took care of these things.

"Okay," said Lucy, leaving her bag on the side of the road and following the boys, who led her past the henhouse, where chickens wandered freely, and on past a large, fenced pasture containing a small herd of goats. The chickens had scooted away from the boys, who Lucy suspected weren't above chasing the birds, but the goats came right up to the fence, rearing onto their hind legs and wagging their little tails. There were a number of adorable little kids gamboling about and even butting each other, and Lucy felt a twinge of sadness for the little males that would most likely have brief lives and end up on the barbecue, sooner rather than later.

The boys scratched the goats on their noses and Lucy did likewise, apologizing to the beasts for not having any treats to give them. "Maybe Mom will give us something for them," suggested Fred, as Lily appeared, coming around a shed and stepping through a gate. She was carrying a large, wooden trug filled with produce, and looked the very picture of a lady gardener, wearing a large straw hat and a pair of denim overalls over a form-fitting, lacy designer T-shirt. Her makeup was perfect, with smoky eyes and glistening coral lips.

"Mom! Can we give something to the goats?" begged Walter.

"Sure." Lily smiled at Lucy. "And who's this?"

"That's Lucy," said Fred. "How about some carrots for the goats?"

"Okay," laughed Lily, handing them a bunch of soil-covered carrots complete with their tops, which they began doling out to the eager goats. She turned to Lucy with an apologetic smile. "Boys will be boys, Lucy. We've been expecting you. I hope you had a smooth crossing."

"It was great," said Lucy. "A beautiful day for sailing."

"That it is," agreed Lily, leading the way

to a path that wound along the western side of the island. "If only every day was as nice as this. It's not so pleasant when there's rain or fog. I hope the weather cooperates while you're with us."

"I'm used to Maine," said Lucy, looking back over her shoulder and finding that her bag had indeed disappeared. Fred was right, someone took care of it. "You know the old saying: If you don't like the weather, wait a minute."

"So true," agreed Lily. "Well, let's get you over to the house and let you get settled. It's a bit of a walk, but the views are fabulous and you'll work up a good appetite. Lunch will be ready in a half hour."

Lucy guessed they'd walked about half a mile when the mansion came into sight. The tall, peaked-roof "cottage" sported new cedar shingles and plenty of gingerbread trim, gleaming with fresh paint. A porch ran around the entire structure, dotted with white wicker furniture. Large, screened windows, open to the breeze, gave glimpses of pine-paneled walls within.

"I just have to drop these veggies off in the kitchen," said Lily. The two women climbed the steps to the porch and went around to the side of the house, where they entered the kitchen, which Lucy noticed had an old-fashioned icebox and a huge black Glenwood range. Susan Hopkins was busy slicing homemade bread for sandwiches, and nodded a greeting as Lily set the trug down on a roomy wood table and continued to lead the way through the antique-filled dining room and hall to the stairs. They climbed up and Lucy was shown to a large, airy room with vintage blue and white wallpaper, white dotted swiss curtains, and a huge, carved wood Victorian bed covered with a patchwork quilt in varying shades of blue.

"This is lovely," exclaimed Lucy.

"It was all here," said Lily, "the wallpaper, the woodwork, even the bed. We just freshened things up a bit, cleaned and oiled the woodwork, that sort of thing. Of course, we got all new mattresses and bedding made from natural fibers, with no nasty chemicals. I hope you'll be comfortable."

"I'm sure I will," said Lucy, noticing that her duffel was waiting for her, set on a bench at the foot of the bed. "Thanks so much for having me."

"The pleasure is ours. Thank you for coming," said Lily, smiling graciously. "Don't forget, lunch in a few minutes."

Lucy found she was in rather dire need of a toilet, after that long sail followed by the

45

walk, and stepped out into the hallway, hoping that Scott Newman's insistence on doing things the old-fashioned way didn't include using an outhouse. Much to her relief she found a large bathroom complete with a footed tub and a flush toilet with a tank high on the wall, which she used. There was even hot water, she discovered when she washed her hands and face, before going downstairs.

Lunch was lively, as Taylor and Parker joined their half brothers and their stepmother at the table, and everyone ate heartily thanks to the invigorating island air. Susan Hopkins had made an assortment of sandwiches: egg salad, cheddar with lettuce and tomato, and a spicy bean spread, followed by a plate of enormous molasses cookies. There was goat's milk for the boys and iced tea for the grown-ups.

"I'm sorry Scott's not here to greet you; he couldn't get away," said Lily, rising from the table and taking the boys off for an hour of quiet time. "I'll let the girls tell you all about their puffin project."

"Your dad mentioned that to me," said Lucy. "What's involved?"

"We have a small breeding colony; it's one of the reasons Dad was so keen on preserving the island," said Taylor. Unlike the boys, the older twins were easier to tell apart. Taylor had freckles and short hair, with blond streaks, and was wearing practical cargo shorts, an oversized Black Dog T-shirt, and Teva sandals.

"We've been monitoring the colony, checking for nestlings and noting how many pairs succeed in raising chicks," said Parker. "The data we collect will be sent to the Audubon Society; they're conducting a worldwide survey. The birds are considered threatened, and the goal is to keep them off the endangered list." Parker had long blond hair, held back with a band, and was wearing short-shorts, a cropped top that revealed a tanned and taut midriff, and wedge sandals.

Remembering Scott's description of his daughters' involvement with his company, Lucy wondered how they managed to spend so much time on the island. "How are you able to be here all summer?" she asked. "You both have important jobs at New World Capital, don't you?"

"Oh, we do," said Taylor. "Parker's a partner, and I'm a VP, I do PR."

"Can you work from here?" she asked, wondering if they communicated by carrier pigeon, or perhaps the puffins took messages back to Boston.

"Dad's got things well in hand," said Parker. "The company goes on summer hours, and what with people's vacations and things, nothing really gets done until September."

"That means we get to work on our tans," said Taylor with a big smile.

"Lucky you," said Lucy, thinking that the girls' jobs were probably honorary titles rather than genuine positions with responsibility. And suspecting they were probably much better compensated than the working stiffs who actually got things done.

The girls drifted off, leaving Lucy alone in the dining room. She decided to use this free time to get the lay of the island and went outside for a self-guided tour. From the porch she could look down to the shore, where a round summer house with a tall, peaked roof overlooked the water. Off to one side of the lawn she noticed an enormous flower garden, bursting with roses, irises, and cosmos. Remembering the trug of garden produce Lily was carrying, Lucy doubted she did much of the actual gardening, that was probably left to the Hopkins boys, or Ben and Wolf. Glancing around at the neatly maintained flower beds bordering the house, and the freshly mowed lawn, Lucy realized that keeping the island in tiptop shape required a lot of work.

Curious about the actual workings of the

island, Lucy wondered where the water system was located that supplied the kitchen and that indoor bathroom, and how it operated. Continuing her exploration and walking to the rear of the house, she found a small windmill turning in the ocean breeze, which was next to a small water tower. She was no hydraulic engineer, but she suspected the windmill pumped groundwater into the tower, where gravity fed it down to the house. That huge woodstove in the kitchen probably also heated the hot water she'd so appreciated when she washed up for lunch.

Continuing around the house, Lucy once again spotted the summer house and decided to check it out. She followed the path that led straight from the house, hinting that it was a popular destination. When she reached it, she discovered why. The structure was much larger than it appeared from the house, and the tall, conical ceiling rose to a great height from which a unique, hand-wrought chandelier was suspended. The sides of the circular building were open to the air and offered panoramic views of the sea. Interestingly, she thought, a staircase along one side seemed to lead down to the shore below.

Following it, she found a lower level that

offered changing rooms, as well as a sturdy door that, when opened, led to a ramp that wound around the structure's foundation and led to the rocks below, which were dotted with tidal pools. Depending on the tide, the pools could be explored for interesting creatures, and the largest ones could even be used for swimming.

Yawning, she decided to rest a bit before ascending the ramp and heading back to the house; she sat down, resting her back against the smooth stone wall of the foundation. It was warm in the sunshine, the rock offered shelter from the wind, and she drifted off. She must have slept for quite a while, because it was the ringing of the dinner gong that finally woke her.

She hurried on up to the lawn, encountering Scott, who said he had just been sailing. "This is the life!" he exclaimed. "Nothing like a sail to work up an appetite!"

"Or a nap in the sun," said Lucy, yawning.

"It's the fresh air, it takes a while to get used to all this oxygen," he said, bounding up the porch steps and holding the screen door open for Lucy. "I've got to clean up, but go on into the living room. I'm sure Lily's got some drinks and appetizers for us."

He pointed the way, through a pair of polished oak doors on the right of the hall, one of which was propped open. Lucy went on in and found a large room with oak wainscoting and a huge stone fireplace. Upholstered wicker furniture was scattered around the room, where Lily was seated by herself on a roomy settee. Parker and Taylor were standing by the fireplace, speaking in low tones, and Lucy sensed a certain tension between the female members of the family.

"Lucy, come sit by me," invited Lily. "Would you like a glass of wine, or something stronger?"

"White wine would be lovely," said Lucy. Lily gave the twins a look, and Taylor pulled herself away from her sister and went to a side table that contained a drinks tray, where she poured a glass of wine for Lucy.

"Perhaps you could bring over that dish of nuts," suggested Lily. Taylor and Parker shared a glance, but Taylor dutifully delivered the wine and nuts, setting them on the wicker coffee table in front of the settee.

"Thanks," said Lucy, raising her glass and taking a sip. She followed this with a nut, which she chewed, trying to think of something to say to Lily. But before she could find a conversational gambit, Scott appeared

51

in the door, radiating energy.

"Fourth of July weekend! And we're all here on the island, celebrating the good old-fashioned way!"

He went straight to the drinks tray, where he fixed himself a stiff scotch on the rocks, then plopped himself down on an easy chair, next to his wife.

"What's the old-fashioned way?" asked Lucy, genuinely curious. There would certainly be no parade on the island, no Boston Pops concert, but might there be fireworks?

"You'll have to wait and see," he teased. "But you can be sure it will be very loud and very illuminating."

"Did you have a smooth sail?" asked Lily.

"Fabulous. I tell you, that boat is a dream, and Will's really coming along. He's a natural sailor." He took a gulp of whiskey and continued, for Lucy's benefit. "She's a thirty-six-foot G L Watson cutter, built in the eighteen nineties and easily handled. One of the few surviving Watsons . . ." He broke off, looking up as Susan appeared in the doorway.

"Dinner is served," she said, turning and going straight back to the kitchen.

"You're in for a treat," Scott told Lucy, as they gathered around the dining table, which was filled with a heaping platter of

52

fish cakes, a casserole of fragrant baked beans, and a huge bowl brimming with salad fixings straight from the garden. "It's all good, wholesome, home-grown fare," he continued. "The earth will provide for us, if we take care of her."

The kitchen door flew open and Susan returned, carrying a pitcher of water, which she set on the table. "Best water in the world," declared Scott, "filtered through native Maine rock, right, Susan?"

"Yes, sir," she replied, before returning to the kitchen. The swinging door closed behind her, and Lucy thought, but couldn't be sure, she heard a derisive snort.

CHAPTER THREE

After dinner, everyone gathered in the living room, where Lily brought out the board games and Scott headed to the drinks table for another scotch on the rocks. The room was cozy, thanks to the glowing lamps and the crackling wood fire, which kept off the evening chill. The boys were keen Monopoly players, and the adults indulged them, allowing them to play as a team. Lucy was amused to see that the twins' approaches to the game were quite different. Walter pursued a business-like strategy of buying up as much property as possible, while Fred was more interested in the riskier approach of picking up Get Out of Jail Free cards. After the boys' shared win, Scott took them up to bed and the women played a game of Scrabble, which Lucy won fair and square.

"I don't know if that was really fair, Lucy," teased Parker, "since you're a professional writer."

"I never think of myself like that," admitted Lucy, who figured her job was mostly a matter of pounding out a story in the fewest and clearest words possible by deadline.

Scott returned, reporting it had been a "three-story bedtime," and went straight to the drinks table again. After he refilled his glass, he went outside to the porch, taking his drink with him.

"This is his quiet time," said Lily with an indulgent smile. "He'll sit out there for hours, staring at the view and the night sky."

"Well, it's a great view," said Lucy, yawning. "I think all this ocean air has done me in. I'll see you in the morning."

"Be sure to take an oil lamp up to bed, the electricity doesn't extend to the second floor," said Taylor. "There's a bunch of them on the hall table by the stairs."

Lucy found the table and chose a lamp, lighting it with one of the provided wooden matches and using it to illuminate her way up the stairs to her room. She washed up in the bathroom, grateful that there was hot water in the main house, even if Wolf's complaint indicated there was none in the workers' quarters. Then she set her flashlight on the night table, got in bed and pulled up the covers, and turned out the oil lamp. At first the room was dark, but when her eyes adjusted she realized that there was a full moon, which gave enough light to make out the shapes in the room. She could see the windows, light-filled rectangles, the dark forms of the dresser and rocking chair, and the footboard of the bed. It was a bit stuffy with the windows closed, so she got out of bed and padded across the room to one of the windows. Shoving the curtain aside, she opened it, letting in the fresh night air. She stood there for a few minutes, taking in the starry sky and the bright moon, thinking of her family at home, of Bill and the girls, of Toby and his family in Alaska, especially little Patrick, and Elizabeth in Paris, and prayed they were all well. Hearing laughter in the distance, she smiled, thinking that someone was having a good time out there. Then she went back to bed, closed her eyes, and immediately fell asleep.

When she woke in the morning, she felt ten years younger and realized it was probably because she'd slept through the entire night for the first time in years. She was usually up at least once, and sometimes more, which she attributed to menopause, but now wondered if it was something else. Maybe it was the stress of modern life, the demands of work, and the evenings spent watching TV that made it impossible for her to get a good night's sleep. Maybe Scott was on to something, she thought, hopping out of bed and going to the window. It was a beautiful morning, clear and sunny, and she decided to forgo her usual morning coffee in favor of a brisk hike around the island. Last night, while playing Scrabble, Parker and Taylor had told her about a trail that wound around the perimeter of the island, and Lucy was eager to find it.

The breeze coming through the open window was cool, so she pulled on jeans and a thick sweatshirt before making a stop in the bathroom to splash some water on her face and brush her teeth. Then she skipped downstairs and, finding the front door locked, went through the kitchen, where she heard Susan clattering pots.

"Coffee's ready," said Susan, when Lucy entered the kitchen.

"I thought I'd go for a walk first," said Lucy. "I'd like to explore the back side of the island and work up an appetite for breakfast."

"Better check the tide table," advised Susan, tilting her head toward a chart that was pinned up on the wall next to the door. "The path dips down from the cliff onto the rocks and it's impassable at high tide."

"Okay," said Lucy, consulting the table.

57

"Today's the second of July and the first high tide is at 11:42 a.m. It's almost seven now, do I have time?"

"Yeah, but you'll want to be on high ground by nine-thirty for sure. It comes in fast, mind."

"I'll keep an eye on the time and the tide," promised Lucy, stepping out onto the porch and into the glorious morning. Following the simple map Parker had drawn for her, she went past the windmill and the water tower, and then continued along a well-trodden path that took her through a pine-woods. The woods were busy with bird activity, and she stopped now and then to observe the chickadees and woodpeckers, birds she recognized, and to try to study and identify the species that were unfamiliar to her. Was that a thrush, a redstart, or a towhee, she wondered, wishing she'd thought to bring her bird book and binoculars.

Eventually the woods thinned out and she found herself on a rocky bluff, high above the blue, blue ocean. Gulls wheeled high above her, calling to each other, and she took a moment to sit on a sun-warmed boulder and just take it all in. Then, mindful of Susan's advice to be wary of the incoming tide, she continued on along the path, which descended to the rocky apron that skirted the island, punctuated here and there with tide pools.

She felt like a little kid again, hopping from rock to rock and pausing to study the creatures trapped in the tide pools: little shrimp that tickled her hand, minnows that darted away from her shadow, and sea urchins and starfish that didn't seem to notice her. There was rockweed, which she recognized, and other seaweeds that she couldn't name in these little ecosystems — tiny, isolated communities that depended on a twice-daily infusion of tidal seawater to bring life-giving nutrients.

Reminded of the tide, Lucy checked her watch and saw it was only a quarter to eight; she had plenty of time. So she poked around a bit longer, inhaling the pungent, ozone-filled air, and listening to the metronomic roar of the encroaching waves that pounded the rocks, the heartbeat of the sea.

As she continued along the rocks, Lucy kept an eye out for the path that Parker had told her last night would lead her back onto high ground, near the puffin breeding colony. Maybe she'd even see some puffins, the comical and colorful sea birds that were said to be related to penguins. She was beginning to worry a bit, minutes were ticking by and there was no sign of a trail on the rocky cliff face, but she did make out something in the distance, lying on the rocks. It was white and caught the light, maybe a marker of some kind?

But as she approached, she realized the shape was no painted rock with a disturbingly human form, it was actually a human. Someone was lying in a very awkward position, and she suspected that person had fallen from the cliff. She began running, intending to help whoever it was and trying to figure out what help she could provide. She was far from the house, and she had no way of communicating and calling for help. Nevertheless, she ran as fast as she could, the pounding surf a reminder that time was running out and the tide was coming in.

She was about a hundred feet away when she could see clearly enough to identify the body. No, she told herself, she didn't want it to be a body. It was a person, a person who needed help. And then there was no denying who it was, and what had happened. It was Parker, and it was obvious that she was beyond help.

Reaching Parker, Lucy fell to her knees. Parker's long blond hair covered her face, and Lucy carefully smoothed it away and studied the girl's face. It revealed nothing;

her eyes were half-closed, her mouth open, giving her a surprised expression. Her hair was dry and fluttering in the wind, now that Lucy had loosened it, but Parker's jeans and sweatshirt were damp. One foot was shod in a sneaker, the other was bare, revealing nails polished in bright pink.

It was the pink painted toenails that undid Lucy, and she sobbed out loud, horrified by the waste, the loss. Poor Parker. A beautiful, privileged, rich young woman with her whole life ahead of her. What happened? How did she end up here, dead on the rocks? A terrible accident? Or was she a victim of murder?

Lucy realized the tide was coming in and she had to get help to recover the body before the tide carried it away. She also knew she was the first, and perhaps only, witness to the death, and she needed to make careful observations. She reached for her cell phone to take pictures, but found her usual pocket was empty. She hadn't brought it because there was no coverage on the island and had packed a digital camera instead, which she hadn't thought to bring and now berated herself for. Stupid! Stupid! All she could do was try to remember as much as she could, and so she tried to shelve her emotions in order to concentrate on the task at hand.

The clothes, her expensive designer sweat-shirt and jeans, were damp, which meant the body had been in the water, but not before high tide, which would have carried it out to sea. She made a quick calculation that high tide must have taken place around eleven o'clock the previous night, so Parker must have fallen to her death several hours later, but before the tide had receded completely, leaving the rocks high and dry.

Lucy studied the corpse carefully, looking for a cause of death, and discovered the back of her head was clearly damaged, indicating a possible fractured skull. Not too bloody, thank goodness, because the receding sea water had washed the gore away. There were other broken bones, too, she decided, observing the awkward ar-rangement of Parker's legs. Maybe a broken arm, too, she thought, noticing how the arm Parker was lying on was twisted beneath her.

Standing up, Lucy brushed away her tears and concentrated hard on studying the face of the cliff. It wasn't sheer rock at this point; there were shrubs and trees that had found a toehold and were growing here and there. Lucy looked for damage, broken branches that indicated Parker might have grabbed at them as she fell, but didn't find any sign that Parker had tried to save herself. It seemed evident that she had been pushed off the top of the cliff with some force, but Lucy wasn't convinced. Maybe the cliff had given way beneath Parker and she'd suddenly found herself falling through thin air. Maybe she'd been partying late into the early hours of the morning and was high on booze or drugs and had stumbled over the edge.

Lucy realized she had found the path to the cliff top and decided she'd better get up it and fast, before the tide came in. She tried to be careful as she climbed, fearful of destroying evidence, but there was no trace of the tragedy on the path. The little, scrubby trees were all intact and when she reached the very top, it was obvious that nothing had been disturbed. There had been no rock fall, no loose sand or gravel that Parker could have slipped on. Lucy paused, surveying the scrubby growth at the top of the cliff, through which the path wandered. She turned back and looked down, for the briefest moment thinking perhaps it had all been a dream, a daydream, some unbidden bit of twisted fantasy. No, she hadn't been making up horror stories; this horror was all too real. Parker was dead and she had to get help, fast, or her body would be carried out to sea and, most probably, never recovered.

She made her way along the path, which circled around an area filled with scrubby plants, as quickly as she could. She assumed it was some sort of puffin nesting area, and she didn't want to disturb the birds, but there was no sign of anything resembling a nest and no birds, either. The day was growing warmer, and she was sweating by the time she reached the shady woods, but she hurried on, jogging along the trail. As she went, she struggled to determine the best way to break the news, as if one way was better than another. No way would be easy, she concluded, but from what she'd observed of the family dynamics, she was certain Scott would want to be the first to know because he would want to take control of the situation.

She struggled along, growing short of breath, and burdened with the terrible news she was bearing. If only she could beam herself up, somehow, and escape this horrible situation. It was only natural, she thought, but nevertheless made her ashamed of herself. She had a terrible task to perform, and she had to do it with the best grace she could muster.

Fortunately, when she reached the house,

she found Scott sitting on the porch outside the kitchen door with a big mug of coffee. "You're up early," he said, smiling with approval. "It's the island, makes you want to get up and get doing. I'm planning to go for a sail. Want to come?"

Lucy stood before him, halfway up the porch steps, trying to catch her breath. Her mind was suddenly blank.

He put down the mug. "Are you okay? Is something the matter?"

"It's Parker." She blurted out the words. "I found her body, on the rocks below the cliff."

For a moment, Scott seemed stunned and didn't move. Finally, he spoke. "Are you absolutely sure?"

Lucy felt tears coming. "I'm so sorry," she said, brushing the tears away.

Scott was immediately on his feet, taking charge. "Don't tell anyone," he said, checking his oversized watch. "I'll get the guys; we have to get her before the tide. Maybe you're wrong, maybe she's alive."

Maybe, thought Lucy, grasping at an irrational little wisp of hope. She nodded, sniffling. "I won't tell anyone."

Then he leaped down the steps, rushing past her in the direction of Ben and Wolf's quarters in the former gardener's cottage.

Lucy grabbed the railing, took a deep breath, and climbed the last few stairs to the porch. It felt like she was climbing Mt. Everest. Moving mindlessly, mechanically, she found herself in the kitchen, where Susan was at the stove, flipping pancakes.

"Are you ready for some breakfast?" she asked.

Lucy stood there, mouth open, trying to think of a reply.

"Goodness, you look like you've seen a ghost!" exclaimed Susan, reaching for the coffeepot. "Here, have a cup of coffee. Sugar? Cream?"

"Thanks," said Lucy, shivering. "I'm cold."

"Here you go." Susan grabbed a sweater from its hook by the door and draped it on Lucy's shoulders, then fixed her a cup of coffee. "Drink this, it'll warm you up."

Lucy lifted the cup and took a sip, swallowed, then felt her stomach heave. She rushed outside and leaned over the porch railing, retching. When it was over, she lifted her head and saw Hopp standing on the lawn, staring at her. "Too much party?" he asked with a knowing grin.

"I guess so," said Lucy, managing a small smile as he passed her on his way to the kitchen.

Following him, intending to retreat to the privacy of her room, she found Hopp whispering with Susan. Noticing her, they gave her a suspicious look, and she decided she'd better stay and pretend everything was normal.

"Sorry about that," she said with a rueful smile. "Do you have any mint tea?"

"Sure thing, honey," said Susan in a motherly tone.

Susan gave Hopp a look and he picked up a large trug from the pile by the door and left, presumably heading for the garden.

The kettle was already on the boil, and Susan fixed a cup of tea for Lucy, urging her to add a lot of sugar. Lucy did, and found the concoction made her feel much better. She was sitting at the big kitchen table, sipping at her tea, when the twin boys clattered in.

"Pancakes!" cried Walter. "My favorite!" added Fred, as they joined her at the table. Susan set big plates of steaming hot cakes in front of them, along with a pitcher of syrup and glasses of milk.

Lily arrived next, wearing what seemed to be her island uniform of a skimpy T-shirt beneath roomy farmer's overalls, her hair perfectly arranged to look casually disarranged, and her face carefully made up complete with shiny lip gloss and smoky eyes. She sat down with a cup of coffee and a small bowl of goat's milk yogurt, which she topped with a dab of maple syrup. "So yummy," she cooed, taking a tiny spoonful.

"Did you sleep well?" she asked Lucy.

"I did," admitted Lucy, thinking that eons must have passed since she awoke.

"That's great, because I want to put you to work. There are goats to milk and eggs to collect."

"I can collect eggs," she said, speaking as if on automatic, "but I've never milked a goat."

"It's easy," promised Lily with a big smile.

"Where's Parker?" asked Fred. "She promised to show me where the redtails have a nest."

This was impossible, thought Lucy, it was all too much. She couldn't sit there with these happy people, knowing what she knew. Knowing that their world was going to come crashing down around them. She wanted to run from the room, screaming and crying, but she couldn't. So she put down her cup, smiled at everyone, and said, "Excuse me. I need to wash up." Then walking stiffly, she left the kitchen and went into the hall. She met Taylor on the stairs, bouncing down with a tennis racquet in her hand, and dashed past, tossing off a brusque "G'morn."

Finally reaching the sanctuary of her room, she threw herself on the bed and buried her face in the pillow, sobbing as if her heart would break. It was more than she could bear, than anyone could bear. Images of Parker's broken body kept flooding in, like a crazy kaleidoscope that shattered into fractions revealing Scott's stone-faced reaction, Lily's brilliant smile, Susan and Hopp's whispering, Taylor's bouncy tennis skirt, and worst of all, little Fred's announcement that Parker was going to show him the hawk's nest.

Finally, the sobs subsided and Lucy turned onto her back, wiping her eyes. That's when she heard a heartrending scream from below, a cry that could split thunder-clouds and shatter mountains.

Rising from her bed, Lucy went to the window. Pushing the lace curtain aside, she looked out and saw the family gathered around a wheeled garden cart containing Parker's body, covered with a tarp. Scott and Lily were standing on either side of Taylor, who had collapsed with grief. She was weeping hysterically and they were embracing her, holding her up. The twin boys, Walter and Fred, looked stunned by the loss of their older sister, and confused by the adults' reactions. The entire Hopkins family was there, too, standing together a bit apart. Will and Brad were looking at their shoes, Hopp was gazing out toward the sea, and Susan was dabbing at her eyes. Standing even farther back, at the edge of the group, she saw Wolf and Ben, looking uneasy, as if they'd like to be somewhere else.

Minutes ticked by and Scott finally pulled himself away from Taylor, leaving her in Lily's arms, resting her head on her stepmother's shoulder. Lily was trying to comfort the grieving girl, murmuring in her ear and smoothing her short hair. Scott conferred briefly with Hopp; then the men arranged themselves on either side of the garden cart and carefully lifted the stretcher containing Parker's body and carried her into the house. The women and boys followed in a sad little procession.

Moments later, she saw Ben and Wolf reappear below her, striding purposefully across the lawn in the direction of the dock, and Lucy assumed they had been dispatched to sail to Tinker's Cove to report the death. As was the case in any unattended death, the medical examiner would have to come and determine the cause of death before issuing a death certificate.

Once again, Lucy wondered if Parker's fall had been accidental, or if she had been pushed. She knew that if the examiner found anything suspicious, there would have to be a police investigation, which would potentially rip apart the tight little island community. The thought disturbed her, and she hoped for everyone's sake that the fall had been the result of an accident.

Then Hopp and his grandsons appeared, gathering briefly in a little huddle. Coming to a decision, they walked off together, in the direction of the farm area. No doubt the animals would need to be fed and watered, and the peas would need to be picked; the death of one human didn't stop nature's relentless cycle of growth and decay.

Remembering that life went on and people would need to be fed and comforted, she went downstairs intending to do whatever she could to help. Susan was standing at the bottom of the stairs and took her hand. "I didn't realize what you'd been through, I'm sorry," she said.

"How could you know?" Lucy patted her hand. "I met Scott outside and told him. He didn't want me to tell anyone else." She sighed. "What can I do to help?"

"The boys," said Susan, "they've kind of

been forgotten. They're sitting outside on the porch steps. . . ."

"I'll take care of them," said Lucy. "I bet they'd like some milk and cookies."

"Good idea," said Susan.

Lucy fetched the boys and brought them into the kitchen, where Susan had put out two glasses of milk and a big plate of molasses cookies. The boys dived in and Lucy took a cookie herself, realizing she hadn't eaten a thing all morning and was very hungry.

"I'm really sorry about Parker," she told them, before biting into the cookie.

"Dad said she fell onto the rocks," said Fred.

"It was an accident," said Walter. "I guess she'll go to heaven."

"No way," said Fred. "Mom said she was a tease; she was mean to the guys."

"Yeah," agreed Walter. "Mom said her shorts were too short."

There it was, thought Lucy, and out of the mouths of babes. The first crack in the illusion of a picture-perfect family life. Of course, all families had their problems, including her own.

"Will they bury her?" asked Walter. "I'd hate to be buried."

"You won't know about it, you'll be dead,"

scoffed Fred.

"How do we know? What if it's a mistake and you're not really dead and you wake up and you're buried?"

"That doesn't happen," said Lucy. "Not ever."

"It could, people wake up from comas," insisted Walter.

"Trust me, dead people don't wake up," said Lucy.

"Why not?" asked Fred.

"They just don't," said Lucy, unwilling to explain the details of the embalming process. "Have another cookie."

"Don't mind if I do," said Walter, sounding a bit like a little old man and making Lucy smile in spite of herself.

For a little while, anyway, thought Lucy, the sunny kitchen seemed removed from the tragedy unfolding on the island. Susan hummed to herself as she made a pot of soup, the boys played tic-tac-toe with Lucy, a cat slept in a sunny spot on the floor. Then there were suddenly raised male voices and Lucy went out to the hall to find out what it was all about.

There she found Ben and Wolf, looking agitated and upset. Scott was coming downstairs, clearly unhappy with the fuss.

"What's going on?" he demanded. "We

finally got Taylor calmed down and now you're making all this noise."

"Sorry, boss," said Ben, "but we got something important —"

"Yeah," Wolf interrupted him. "The boats are gone."

"What do you mean?" demanded Scott.

"The boats." Wolf spoke slowly. "They're not there."

"The Watson is gone? What about the catboat?"

"No sign of them, boss," said Ben.

"Didn't you tie them up properly?" Scott was immediately accusative.

"Sure thing," reported Ben. "Checked them last night. All safe and secure."

Scott was not convinced. "Well, get out a dinghy and go look for them. They can't have got far."

Ben and Wolf were headed for the door when it flew open and Brad dashed in, breathless, capturing everyone's attention. What next, wondered Lucy. What else could go wrong?

"The boats!" he exclaimed.

"Yeah, I know they're gone," said Scott. "Get a move on and start looking for them."

"No need," said Brad. "They drifted off and smashed to bits on Whale Point. I saw some flotsam and went to investigate.

They're ruined."

"Smashed to bits," repeated Scott, stunned. "How can that be?"

"The surf's high there, nothing could survive that pounding," said Brad. "There's nothing worth saving. They're gone. Wrecked."

"Not my cutter," said Scott, shaking his head in denial. "Not the Watson."

"Both of them, the cat and the cutter," said Brad.

"That's unbelievable." Scott sat down hard on a stair. "Where's Will?" he asked.

"He's headed for the Point. I told him it was useless, but he said he had to go."

"Yeah," agreed Scott. "Maybe we can salvage something. Get ropes, hooks, anything you can think of."

Wolf and Ben shared a glance, acknowledging the futility of the effort, but offered no resistance. Brad, on the other hand, voiced his reluctance. "It's no good. There's nothing we can do. The surf is too strong there."

"I have to see for myself," insisted Scott, rising to his feet. "Let's go."

He led the way, followed by the others, and as she watched the somber procession, Lucy thought it was as if there'd been another death on the island.

Chapter Four

Lucy's first reaction was to share the news with Susan, and to learn what the loss of the boats meant. Were they completely cut off from civilization? Was there a way to signal for help? Could a couple of the guys row the ten miles over to Tinker's Cove, relying on grit, determination, and muscle power to overcome the notorious currents? And bubbling away underneath all her questions was the growing suspicion that Parker's death had not been accidental at all, but had been committed by someone who was determined to get away with murder.

She didn't share her suspicions with Susan, of course, but merely told Susan that the boats had been wrecked on the rocks. "What does that mean?" she asked.

"It means somebody doesn't know how to tie a decent knot," said Susan with a snort. "Not my boys, that's for sure." She paused. "It's a shame, though. That yacht of Scott's is, I guess it's *was* now, was a real beauty. You say they're past repairing?"

"That's what Brad said. Smashed to bits."

The twins were listening intently, and Susan brusquely ruffled their hair. "When it rains, it pours." She looked out the window, checking the sky, and made a funny little "humpf" sound, then smiled at the boys. "It's no matter, really. The state ferry is due in a few days, and until then we'll be fine. Why, in the old days the islanders were cut off for months at a time, especially in winter. They had to be self-sufficient, and your dad has followed in their footsteps. We'll be fine, you'll see." She picked up the empty plates and glasses, setting them in the sink. "Meanwhile, why don't you boys go out and pick some flowers for your mom. She loves roses, and I saw that yellow bush is covered with flowers."

"Okay," said Walter.

"Be careful, mind the thorns," advised Susan, giving him a pair of clippers and choosing the smallest trug, which she handed to Fred.

Lucy watched them leave, feeling a bit uneasy. "Will they be okay on their own?" she asked.

"Why ever not?" replied Susan. "They know every inch of this island."

"Right," answered Lucy, who wasn't really worried about the dangers posed by the island, but rather by its inhabitants. "I think I'll go help them, make sure they pick the best ones."

"No, they'll be fine, and I need you to help me lay out the body." She nodded. "Now that we're cut off we'll have to keep her for a few days, you know, and in this weather it's best for everyone if we get her cleaned up and put on ice."

Lucy's first reaction was to refuse. "Sorry, but I cannot help you, not with that. I wouldn't know where to begin." She shook her head. "And besides, we'd be destroying evidence. The medical examiner will be conducting an autopsy. . . ."

Susan gave her a withering look. "It needs to be done."

"Well, I'm not going to be part of it. That poor girl deserves a thorough investigation. What if her death wasn't an accident?"

"Of course, it was an accident," snapped Susan. "Think of the family. We can't leave her lying there on the dining room table, not in this heat."

It was true, admitted Lucy. Something had to be done with Parker's body. "Okay," she said, aware that despite her horror at the no doubt gruesome task, she felt a growing curiosity. What exactly was laying out? How did you do it? And would it reveal evidence that pointed to murder? Evidence that could be preserved?

"It's been some time since I laid out a body," said Susan. "My mum taught me, back in the day, when there was a real community on the island. No proper undertaker, though, so we had to do it ourselves. A good number of folks are buried here in the old graveyard. Not all, o'course. Plenty was lost at sea. Never recovered."

"That must have been hard," said Lucy, thinking about the graveyard in Tinker's Cove. There the tombstones told a tale of hard times, before vaccines and antibiotics, when entire families were wiped out with fever in a matter of weeks. There were so many little babies, many not even named, along with their mothers, who died in childbirth or soon after from childbed fever. She'd also noticed the graves of several sea captains who were buried alongside a succession of wives. But men were also subject to early death; there were plenty of young fellows who survived the dangers of eighteenth- and nineteenth-century childhood only to die in battle or at sea. "Lost in fog," was a common epitaph.

"Time's a'wastin', this isn't getting the

job done," said Susan, suddenly all business, instructing Lucy to go to the linen closet next to the bathroom, where she would find sheets and towels. She was to bring these down to the dining room, and when she returned she found Susan lowering the window shades. "Don't want anybody looking in," she told Lucy.

Then Susan spread out a sheet on the table and covered it with several towels, readying it to receive the body. That task done, Susan went upstairs to Parker's room to get clean clothes and a hairbrush. When she returned, Susan lifted the blue poly tarp, which crackled, and handed it to Lucy. "Fold this up," she said, and Lucy obliged, all the time looking at Parker. Nothing had changed, the girl was still in the jeans and sweatshirt Lucy had found her in, and the missing sneaker was still missing. Her long hair was sprayed out beneath her head, and her face had the same expression of surprise.

"We're going to undress her and then shift her body onto the towels," said Susan, prompting Lucy to stop staring and get on with the task of folding the tarp.

Susan unzipped the sweatshirt, revealing a white jersey camisole beneath. It was clear as she struggled to remove the sweatshirt that rigor was setting in; Parker's limbs were somewhat stiff and unyielding. In the end she cut the sleeves and had Lucy lift the corpse so she could slide the thick sweatshirt off. Then she slit the cami's side seams, and they slipped it over her head to remove it.

Lying there, half dressed, Parker was looking more like a corpse in a detective show than a person. Her skin was waxy, her breasts had fallen to either side, her arms were bruised. Her manicure, however, had stood up just fine, which Lucy took to be evidence that she had not tried to save herself when she fell.

Susan unzipped the jeans, which they managed to tug off with difficulty, but without cutting. A snip or two of the scissors and Parker's lacy thong underpants came right off. Lucy noticed that the left leg was obviously broken, which she had guessed was the case when she discovered the body.

"Now we move her," said Susan, grabbing Parker beneath her shoulders. Lucy took the feet and with a one-two-three they heaved her onto the towels. Lucy was told to fold up her clothes and put them aside, while Susan carefully washed and dried the body, and gently tucked cotton balls into the various body orifices. The long hair was matted and tangled, and as she gently brushed it she clucked her tongue. "Look at that, poor girl never had a chance."

Lucy looked and saw how the back of Parker's skull was misshapen. "Touch it," urged Susan, and when she did, she recoiled.

"Mushy, isn't it?" said Susan, as if noting an interesting phenomenon.

Lucy nodded and swallowed hard, willing herself not to retch.

Setting the brush aside, Susan pointed to the two garments she had brought from Parker's room. One was the flowery shift Lucy saw her wearing the night of the party; the other was a white eyelet with long sleeves and a front zipper, which Lucy suspected was probably a beach cover-up.

"I think the white would be easier, thanks to the zip," she suggested, and Susan nodded in agreement.

Together they managed the awkward business of dressing the body and returning it to the backboard. When they'd finished, Susan began humming "Amazing Grace" as she fussed, arranging the arms and legs as best she could. Then she took a long strip of gauze and looped it under Parker's chin, tying it in a neat bow on top of her head. She produced two quarters from a jar she kept in the pantry, and used them to close the girl's eyes, adding a tiny bit of adhesive tape to keep them in place. Finishing the tune, she sighed. "I guess that's all we can do," she said with a sigh. Then she unfolded a sheet and carefully laid it over the body, tucking it in all around.

"I think the boys can put her in the icehouse," she said. "I think she'll keep all right until the ferry comes."

Lucy nodded, thinking Susan made poor Parker sound like a piece of meat she was planning to serve in a few days' time. Overcome with emotion, and exhaustion, she collapsed onto one of the dining chairs, staring at the sheeted body. A body that was once a beautiful, living, breathing young woman. A girl not unlike her own daughters, who were just getting started on adult life. Sara and Zoe were still in college, busy with summer jobs and friends, while also fretting over course choices and grades, and considering various careers. Elizabeth, her oldest daughter, was well on her way, with an exciting job in Paris as a concierge at the toney Cavendish Hotel there. They were all fit and healthy, but Lucy knew that could change in an instant. There were terrorists and mass shooters, there was cancer and automobile accidents, dangers all around, especially for young women. A date could turn into rape, or even murder. A husband or boyfriend could become a killer. She'd covered too many stories about wives and sisters and daughters whose bodies were dumped alongside the highway, left on the bed, mangled and tossed into Dumpsters. She'd interviewed their grieving families, she'd seen their accused murderers in court. She closed her eyes and prayed for her own girls' safety, and for the safety of all women.

Her prayer was interrupted when Susan announced that the body was ready, and now the family could say their goodbyes to Parker.

"Is that really a good idea?" asked Lucy, who was shocked at the idea. To her mind, the dear departed should be remembered in the abstract, as "those we love but see no longer" and not as inanimate corpses. "Think of what they must be going through right now, especially the boys."

Susan raised her eyebrows. "Well, I never. Of course, they'll want to see her and know she's gone and say their farewells." She snorted. "Better now than in a few days, believe me."

"I guess you're right," admitted Lucy, as Susan bustled out to organize the viewing. It was true that no funeral could take place until a death certificate was issued, and that couldn't happen until the ferry arrived and the medical examiner was summoned. Once again it occurred to her that Scott's plan to shun the trappings of modern life, including communication, was rather foolhardy. The simple life wasn't really simple at all, it was fraught with unforeseen challenges and difficulties, as the present situation clearly showed. She wondered if Scott was wishing he had a working cell phone; she wondered if he might be thinking of modifying his resistance to electronic devices.

As she sat there, she began to wonder if it was appropriate for her to stay during what would surely be an intimate family moment. She sensed that she really ought to leave, that would be the proper thing to do. On the other hand, however, witnessing the viewing might give her an insight into the Newman family dynamics, and maybe even a clue that would explain Parker's death. No, she decided, coming down on the side of discretion, if indeed there was anything suspicious about Parker's death, it would surely come out in the next few days. She stood up, intending to leave, when Susan returned.

"Oh, good, you're still here," she said, handing her a box of tissues. "I think they might need some support."

"Is Scott back?" asked Lucy. "He went to the Point to see the damage to the boats."

"He just came in, looks like death himself," said Susan.

Lucy nodded and stepped back, toward a corner, still holding the tissues. The door opened and Scott entered, followed by Lily and the boys. Taylor trailed behind, clearly the most upset member of the family, looking quite shaken and drawn. Lucy knew that twins were supposed to be especially close, so Taylor's extreme grief was understandable. What was rather more confusing was the way Scott ignored his daughter, focusing instead on supporting his wife. That was all wrong, thought Lucy, watching as he wrapped his arm around Lily's waist and drew her close to himself. Lily wasn't even Parker's real mother; she was only a few years older than Parker and probably saw her stepdaughter as a rival for her husband's affection. Then she mentally scolded herself, remembering that Scott himself must be suffering and had turned to his wife for comfort.

Stepping into the void, she took Taylor's hand and the girl managed to give her a small smile. She felt Taylor's body stiffen as Susan stepped closer to the covered body, where she prepared to lift the sheet shrouding Parker. She waited a moment, until she received a nod from Scott, then folded the sheet back, revealing Parker's face.

Concerned that the sight might be too much for the twin boys, Lucy took her hand away from Taylor's and stepped toward them, intending to stand behind them and give their shoulders a squeeze. It was then that Taylor tumbled to the floor in a dead faint.

Parker was forgotten and everyone turned to Taylor. She was lying on her back and was already stirring when Lucy knelt beside her. "Take your time," she urged. "You fainted."

"I fainted?"

"It happens," said Lucy, helping her to sit up. "How do you feel?"

"A bit woozy," admitted Taylor.

"Take it easy," advised Lucy.

"Always jealous," snapped Scott. "Always upstaging your sister, even now."

Lily gave her husband a disapproving look and took Taylor's hand. "Upsa daisy," she said, as she and Lucy helped the girl to her feet and set her on a chair. "I think we're done here. There's nothing we can do to change the past, what's done is done. Parker knows she was loved, that's the important thing."

She took her boys by the hand and led them out of the dining room. Taylor got to her feet and followed, a bit unsteadily. Only Scott remained, staring down at his daughter's expressionless face. He touched her hair and bent, planting a kiss on her forehead. "Bye, bye, sweetgums," he said, then replaced the sheet over her face.

Susan opened the porch door and the four young men came in. Scott stood aside while they lined up two by two on either side of the backboard containing the shrouded body, then lifted it and carried it out of the kitchen. Scott followed as they went across the porch and down the steps, and placed it again on the wheeled garden cart.

Lucy and Susan stood together on the porch, watching, as the men began the half-mile walk to the icehouse. Ben and Wolf each took one of the cart's handles, and Will and Brad walked alongside, making sure the body didn't slip. Scott followed, a solitary mourner in the sad procession.

"He loved that girl," said Susan, turning and going back into the kitchen. Lucy remained on the porch, her mind a jumble of thoughts and emotions. Maybe it was all just a coincidence, but it seemed extremely odd that the boats had been destroyed so soon after Parker's death. Maybe they hadn't been properly tied by one of the guys who was in a hurry or distracted, or maybe the twins had untied them in a bit of mischief. Or maybe, she thought, they had been set loose by a murderer intent on delaying any investigation.

CHAPTER FIVE

Why kill Parker? That was the thing that Lucy simply couldn't wrap her mind around, as she remained on the porch, unable to decide what to do with herself. She was in a horribly awkward position as the guest of a family dealing with a tragic loss. Even worse, she was a journalist, a professional snoop. If things had been different, she could have discreetly departed, leaving the Newmans to mourn in privacy. But here she was, stranded until the state ferry made its monthly stop, plunk in the middle of what she knew was going to be a huge story.

She thought what Ted's reaction would be if she told him she had decided not to investigate Parker's death because she felt it would be impolite and intrusive. She was a reporter, here on assignment, and even though the story was not developing as she expected, she had a duty to follow where it led. And that meant finding out how Parker had died, and why.

That reminded her of a comment, made by one of her favorite fictional sleuths, that it was futile to speculate about a murderer's motive, that the motive only became clear once the killer was identified. It was more productive, claimed the detective, to focus on means and opportunity rather than to waste time speculating on possible motives.

Maybe so, admitted Lucy, but she couldn't help wondering why Parker was killed. If indeed she was killed, which was an open question. Her death might have been accidental, but the fact that the boats had been destroyed argued against that theory. Or maybe, thought Lucy, the fall hadn't been caused intentionally but had taken place during an argument due to a shove, or a misstep. Perhaps she'd been trying to avoid an unwanted embrace, something like that.

She thought of Zoe's new love interest, Mike Snider, and frowned, staring at the ocean view and thinking of home, ten miles away across the water. Zoe didn't seem interested in avoiding Mike's embraces, despite her parents' disapproval. If anything, Lucy suspected that their disapproval made him even more desirable. Though what Zoe saw in him was more than Lucy could fathom since, in her eyes, he was lazy, slovenly, and rude. Finding him rooting about in the refrigerator and taking one of Bill's favorite craft beers had shocked Lucy to the core. Nobody did that! Next thing he'd be poking in the medicine cabinet, helping himself to whatever he fancied: dental floss, painkillers, or that expensive allergy nasal spray. The thought of him shoving the applicator into his hairy nose made Lucy cringe.

But none of the four young men on the island were like Mike Snider, she thought, with a sense of relief. They were all well-mannered and attractive — or were they? Maybe they were just good actors, playing the part of helpful, eager workers. Which was exactly what Ben and Wolf seemed as they made their way across the grassy lawn, approaching the house. When they reached the porch, they paused to greet her with nods and small smiles before climbing the steps and continuing into the house. Moments later, Scott appeared, marching across the lawn and onto the porch, ignoring her completely.

Lucy watched as they gathered in the hall, wondering what was going on. Did they come to discuss a mutual discovery or decision? Or had Ben and Wolf been summoned, called on the carpet? Curious to learn more, she followed them to the doorway, but stopped short of entering when she heard Scott's voice sharply ordering them into the dining room. She didn't want to be caught eavesdropping, so she wandered around the porch to the side of the house, where a wicker divan had been placed beneath the dining room windows. She decided to sit there and pretend to read one of the magazines that had accumulated on a side table.

Once settled with last month's *Vogue,* she discovered that the open window allowed her to hear everything that was said inside. "You were supposed to make sure the boats were secure, that was your job," said Scott, putting the two on the spot. "What happened?"

There was a long silence; then Ben spoke. "The boats were secure last time I checked."

"And when was that?" demanded Scott.

"Last night, before I turned in."

"Last night! What about this morning? Were they there this morning? Did you notice? Did you check?"

"Not me," said Wolf. "Ben was up before me and I figured he'd done it."

"And did you?" Lucy couldn't see the men, but in her mind's eye Scott must have turned to Ben.

"I didn't have a chance. I was just washing up when you came and got us. I went and got Wolf; we were all in a rush to help Parker."

There was a long pause; then Scott asked, "So when did you first notice the boats were gone?"

"We came and told you right away," said Ben.

"It was twenty past nine, I checked my watch," said Wolf.

"Well, that's something, thanks," said Scott, somewhat mollified. "You can go, but keep an eye out. I don't want to be paranoid, but considering what's happened we've got to be realistic." He paused. "I have enemies, you know. You can't be successful without stepping on a few toes, and there's plenty who'd like to get back at me: competitors, disgruntled employees, dissatisfied investors. Let me know if you notice anything out of the ordinary, okay?"

"Okay, boss," said Ben.

"Will do," said Wolf.

Moments later, Lucy heard the screen door slam and saw the two men striding off. She was getting up, intending to go to her room, when she was surprised by Scott, who had stepped outside onto the porch.

"Ah, Lucy." He seemed ill at ease, as if struggling to think what to say next.

"I'm very sorry," said Lucy, saying the first thing that came into her head. "I'd like to help any way I can."

"You've already been a great help," he said. "It's thanks to you we were able to recover Parker's, um, body . . . an hour later and she would have been carried out to sea."

"Well, I'm glad for that."

"And I know you helped Susan with the . . . with the . . ."

"The laying out," said Lucy in a soft voice. "It was an honor to do what little I could."

"Now all we can do is wait for the ferry." He snorted. "That's going to be the hardest part. I hate waiting."

"Is there no way you can call for help?" asked Lucy.

"No." It was a one-syllable bark, a snap.

"Well, then, we have to make the best of it and help each other."

"A tight little island."

Seeing her puzzled expression, he continued. "My grandparents used to talk about this old movie about an island, it was called *Tight Little Island.* I loved the way they used to say it and laugh, like it was a private joke. It made me want to live on an island, it seemed to me it would be a happy, safe place. That's all I wanted this to be, a shelter, a refuge for my family. A place to be happy together." He snorted. "I was wrong about it all, even about the movie. It wasn't at all what I thought. I stumbled on it one night, late on one of those classic movie channels. It was made sometime around World War II, a grainy old black and white about a ship full of whiskey that gets torpedoed and all the booze floats onto this remote British island. I was thinking Bobbsey Twins or the Five Little Peppers, and it wasn't like that at all. It was about a bunch of drunks. I couldn't even understand half of what they were saying, the accents were so thick."

"In my experience," said Lucy, "things rarely turn out as we expect." She sighed. "If there's anything I can do, just ask."

"Thanks, Lucy." He turned and went back into the house, and when Lucy followed she saw him in the living room, pouring himself a whiskey from the bar in the corner. Tight little island indeed, she thought, at least for him.

The house suddenly seemed oppressive to Lucy, who imagined the various members of the family closeted behind closed doors with their grief. What about the boys, she wondered, hoping their mother was giving them the love and support they needed. This was ideally a time for the family to draw together, but Lucy knew that tragedy sometimes had the opposite effect and ripped families apart, revealing tensions and conflicts that had been simmering beneath the surface. She feared an emotional storm might be about to break in this handsome old mansion and decided to clear out for a while, hoping to avoid it.

Stepping onto the porch, Lucy noticed a temporary darkness as a cloud briefly covered the sun, and she felt a change in the air as the refreshing morning breezes were replaced by still, oppressive air. Glancing skyward, she saw that clouds were piling up and beginning to fill the sky, which was growing grayer by the minute. Not a good sign, she thought, heading along the perimeter path past the old gardener's cottage, where Ben and Wolf were quartered, and continuing past the decrepit, unrestored greenhouse and on toward the dock. Much to her surprise, Ben was standing there, alone, looking out to the gray sea with his hands in the pockets of his cargo shorts.

"A penny for your thoughts," said Lucy, climbing up the step or two that led to the dock.

"Not printable," said Ben, greeting her

with a wry smile.

"Oh, anything goes these days," she replied, thinking of the supermarket tabloids that were notorious for their outrageous, attention-grabbing headlines. The *Pennysaver,* on the other hand, was a family newspaper, as Ted was always reminding her. She stepped beside him and squinted into the distance, making out the low gray shape of the mainland on the horizon. "I wish I was over there," she said, "instead of here."

"Me too," said Ben, with a big sigh.

"You're from Brooklyn, right?" again asked Lucy.

"Yeah."

Lucy had recently visited Brooklyn and knew that gentrified borough was a magnet that attracted the young and hip. "Why on earth did you leave Brooklyn for this isolated island?" she asked, puzzled.

"A friend of mine got hired and convinced me to come, too. Said it would get us out of the city for the summer, and we'd get good pay. It sounded like a sweet deal, so I applied and got the job. Then my friend took another job, closer to home out on Montauk. Go figure."

"I've been to Brooklyn." Lucy thought of her friend Sue's daughter, Sidra, who also

lived in Brooklyn, in a Park Slope brown-
stone on a leafy, crowded street. "I didn't
see many boats there except ferries."

"Well, there are. The Navy Yard is there,
the East River, the harbor, there's a lot of
marine activity. I was working on a water
taxi, you know, like a cab but on the river.
I've got a captain's license and everything."

"I stand corrected," said Lucy, smiling.
"So what happened to the boats?"

"I wish I knew." He gazed off toward
Whale Point, where the surf pounded
against the rocks and the breaking waves
produced huge showers of spray. "The current is killer here, it would have carried
them off in no time."

"Why did they put the dock here?" asked
Lucy. "Isn't there a calmer spot?"

"I don't think so, this here is actually
pretty calm, protected by the Point." He
was thoughtful. "There's really no good
place on this island, it's just the way it is.
There's submerged outcrops out there; you
can't see them, but they're marked with
those buoys, right? The current is pushed
between them and the island; it creates a lot
of force, kind of like a whirlpool, even
though this is the leeward side. It's deceiv-
ing."

Lucy looked where he was pointing and

noticed several buoys, bobbing in the near distance. "Oh," she exclaimed, "that's why there's so little boating traffic out here. I wondered why we don't see lobster boats or pleasure craft."

"Yeah, nobody wants to mess with the current unless they've got a reason to get here and since the island is private, there's no reason."

Turning back toward the island, she noticed a flag flying on a pole next to the boathouse. The flag bore the same white Quahog Republic logo that was on Ben's black T-shirt.

"How serious is Scott about this Quahog Republic stuff?" she asked with a smile. "Wolf said it's kind of a joke, right?"

"No joke. It's Scott's notion of his own little island, like it's his country or something and he's the president." He paused, then added, "Not exactly president, better make that king, or even dictator."

Lucy was thoughtful. "Why not turn it upside down? Isn't that an international distress signal?"

"I suggested it, but Scott said no." He shrugged. "Probably wouldn't matter. It's not a widely recognized image. I doubt anybody would realize if it was right side up or upside down."

"Isn't there an American flag somewhere? That would be recognizable."

"Yeah," said Ben, "but this isn't America. It's the Quahog Republic and Scott's flying his flag, no matter what."

"Right." Lucy felt very tired. It had been a long day, even though it wasn't even lunchtime. She was growing increasingly frustrated by the limits Scott imposed in his little dictatorship: no cell phones, no TV, no radio, limited electricity. It was ridiculous to shun these conveniences, as the present situation clearly showed. And what if Parker hadn't died, but needed emergency medical attention? What if one of the boys got sick? It would be heartbreaking if Walter or Fred fell ill from appendicitis or something and died due to the difficulty of getting prompt medical care. It occurred to her that Scott really hadn't thought this through. His idea of creating a refuge, a safe island for his family, was actually putting them in danger.

"He's crazy," said Ben, echoing her thoughts. "Out of his effing mind. He won't even let the Hopkinses moor their lobster boat on the island. He told them it was too smelly and noisy. So if they want to pull pots, they've got to sail over to Tinker's Cove, adding hours to an already long day. They're pretty much giving up, that's what

Brad told me."

"What's going on with them?" asked Lucy. "I can't imagine they're very happy about Scott's changes."

"I'm not so sure about that. They've always been here, families have been on the island for centuries. They're kind of into the rugged, independent Maine thing, tougher than nails, something like that."

Lucy found herself laughing. "And I suppose he pays them well."

"I think so. Face it, there were no jobs on the island before Scott. It was a hardscrabble existence, depending on the lobsters and what they could grow. Susan used to knit baby sweaters and sold them at some craft co-op. She told me she's too busy now, what with all the cooking and cleaning, but she also said she doesn't need the cash because she's getting paid by Scott. If you ask me, I think they've suddenly got more money than they know what to do with." He snorted. "You sure can't spend it here, can you?"

Lucy thought about how isolated the island was, how cut off from the rest of the world, and remembered something she'd overheard Scott saying. Unwilling to admit she'd been eavesdropping, she referred to an imaginary conversation. "When I was talking to Scott," she fibbed, "he seemed to imply that perhaps some intruders had come to the island. Do you think that's possible?"

"Yeah, he told Wolf and me to keep our eyes out for something like that, but they would have to be Navy Seals to make it to the island without being discovered. I guess that's possible, maybe some James Bond–type villain who has a private army of mercenaries or something, but I kinda doubt it." He bit his lip. "I hate to say it, but I think that if there is some sort of evil afoot and this isn't all a series of unfortunate coincidences, it's gotta be one of us. And it follows that I'm the only one of us who's kind of different. I'm clearly Latino, right, with my skin and hair and accent. I can even speak Spanish; I had to if I was going to talk to my grandparents. They barely knew any English. So here I am, the odd one out, and it's just a matter of time before somebody accuses me."

"You can't really think that," said Lucy.

"Of course, I do. It's self-preservation. Take those girls, for example. Taylor and Parker. They've got a whole island at their disposal, including that fancy gazebo bathhouse, but what did they do? They'd come down to the dock in skimpy bikinis my sister would not be caught dead in. . . ." He caught himself too late. "Well, you know what I mean. Like string bikinis. And they'd spread out towels and lie down and sun themselves on the dock. They'd take off the tops and lie there, like they were all alone and nobody could see. Except, of course, they knew we were here, all of us guys, and they sure wanted us to notice them."

"Did any of you do more than notice?"

"Not that I know of, and definitely not me. No way I was going to get involved," he said with a knowing nod. He turned and strode off along the dock, hopping down easily onto the ground and disappearing into the boathouse. Lucy remained a few minutes, thinking over what he had said, then decided to go back to the house. It was growing chilly, now that the sun had gone, and she needed a sweater.

CHAPTER SIX

The twins were kicking a soccer ball around on the lawn when Lucy got back to the house. She had just passed the big flower garden when the ball came her way and she kicked it back to Fred. Even from across the lawn she knew it was Fred because she recognized the blue polo shirt he was wearing. She continued on her way, but he kicked the ball at her again, and this time she sent it sailing to Walter. Back it came and before she knew it, she was drawn into their game. It wasn't something she normally did, having left the youth sports side of parenting to Bill. He was the one who ran around on the lawn after dinner, giving Toby tips on batting and fielding when he was in Little League, and urging Elizabeth to "show some hustle" during the one season she reluctantly played field hockey. Lucy smiled, remembering how Elizabeth had finally given in, but only because she thought the kilts were cuter than soccer shorts. Both Sara and Zoe enjoyed soccer, and Bill learned the sport along with the girls, volunteering as a coach for the six-year-olds and moving up the ranks with them. But Lucy had limited her involvement to arriving a few moments before the practice or game was scheduled to end and either congratulating them on a win or consoling them for a loss while driving them home. But today, she found herself enjoying the game. It felt good to run after the ball, with no thought except giving it a good, sound kick and sending it flying. Most times the boys were able to stop it, but she got a few by them. When she missed a ball, or attempted a kick that missed, they would laugh and tease her for being clumsy.

"Time for lunch," she said, when Fred kicked the ball especially hard and sent it soaring across the lawn and right over the fence into the garden, where it got lost amid the thorny rosebushes.

"Yeah, we can look for it later," said Fred, taking her hand.

"I'm hungry," added Walter, taking her other hand.

Lucy was hungry, too, and checking her watch she saw it was well past one o'clock and there had been no sign of lunch. "Let's see what I can find for us to eat," she said, leading the way.

Walking together toward the house, both boys leaned against her, seeking physical contact. Nobody had been paying any attention to them, she realized, and they desperately needed adult support and guidance to help them cope with the loss of their older sister. She guessed this was their first experience with the death of a loved one, and Parker hadn't been the usual aged grandparent but a young and vital sister. It was a lot for two little boys to come to terms with, and Lucy hoped their parents would realize how deeply they were affected. Of course, Scott and Lily had to manage their own deep grief, and it would be easy to focus on the boys' youthful energy and miss the fact that they were also grieving and needed special attention.

The kitchen was unoccupied when they stepped inside, so Lucy got busy slicing bread and making hearty peanut butter and jelly sandwiches. She filled big glasses with goat's milk and even found a few remaining molasses cookies in the jar, which she put on a plate. When she brought the food to the table, she was happy to see the boys were giggling about something.

"What's so funny?" she asked, taking a seat.

The two looked at each other, laughed, and then Walter confessed all. "We saw Parker's bum," he said, setting off another round of giggles.

For a moment Lucy was horrified; had they seen Parker's body when she and Susan were laying her out? "When was this?" she asked in the most nonchalant tone she could manage.

Walter was busy chewing, so Fred answered. "The other day."

"Oh," said Lucy, picking up her sandwich and taking a small bite.

"At the pond," added Walter, with a full mouth.

"Don't talk with your mouth full," she said. "And you know you shouldn't spy on people, right?"

"We weren't spying, we were hunting for frogs," said Fred.

"Where is this pond?" asked Lucy, curious.

"On the other side of the farm," said Walter in a tone that implied she should have known.

"I suppose she was swimming," said Lucy. "Lots of people like to skinny-dip."

"She wasn't swimming," said Walter, who

had taken another bite of sandwich and had a bit of trouble getting the words out.

"Really, Walter, you shouldn't talk with your mouth full," said Lucy. She waited until he'd swallowed, and continued. "What was she doing, if she wasn't swimming?"

"She was lying on a blanket with Will," said Fred.

Lucy almost spit out the milk she was drinking, but managed to swallow instead. "Went down the wrong way," she explained between coughs.

"Yeah, I thought Will was supposed to be working," said Fred, apparently eager to be his father's overseer, keeping an eye on the hired help.

"Maybe Parker asked him to do something, like help her put on some sunblock, or kill a bug," suggested Lucy, expressing solidarity with the working class.

"Maybe," admitted Fred, reaching for a cookie.

"Maybe," agreed Walter, before eating the last bite of sandwich and earning an approving smile from Lucy. "Say, do you want to hunt for frogs with us?" he asked.

"We'll see," said Lucy, who was thinking about the social structure on the island, and wondering about the relationships between employers and employees, old-timers and newcomers. If only she were a sociologist, she mused, it would probably make an interesting study.

"Can I have some more milk?" asked Walter, whose glass was empty and who was starting in on his enormous cookie.

"Absolutely," said Lucy, getting up and going to the ice box. "How about you, Fred?"

"I'd like some, too," he said, taking the last cookie.

Lucy was bringing the pitcher to the table when the swinging door flew open and Lily flew in, suddenly recollecting her motherly responsibilities. She'd changed out of the casual overalls she'd been wearing earlier and was now dressed in skinny black slacks and a fluttery white chiffon blouse.

"Oh, my boys," she cooed, scooping first Fred and then Walter in big hugs. "You're being so brave."

Taking in the empty plates and glasses, and Lucy herself, who was standing in the middle of the kitchen with the milk pitcher, Lily decided congratulations were in order. "You've had lunch, how wonderful. Thank you, Lucy. You're a wonder. And you boys, you're such little men. . . ." Then her voice broke and she burst into tears, running from the room.

"Mom seems upset," said Fred in a philosophical tone of voice.

"Yeah, I didn't know she even liked Parker," said Walter, sounding puzzled.

"Yeah," added Fred. "She must've changed her mind, now that Parker's dead."

"Why would she do that?" wondered Walter.

"I dunno," said Fred. "Grown-ups are weird."

"Let's see if we can find some frogs eggs," suggested Walter. "We can put 'em in a jar and see if they hatch."

"Okay."

The two boys went out, leaving Lucy alone in the kitchen. She started clearing the table, carrying the dishes to the sink for washing. No dishwasher, she thought, filling the dishpan with sudsy water and using the old-fashioned dishmop to wash the dishes, which she decided was kind of fun. Like water play, or blowing bubbles, but not really practical for a busy household like hers.

Households, she thought, wondering about the Newman family. She thought about Lily, wondering what sort of stepmother she was. Was she kind and loving, and really and truly upset about Parker's death, or was she more like the fairy tale stepmothers who plotted against their stepchildren? According to the twins, Lily hadn't bothered to hide her dislike of Parker, but from the way she was crying and carrying on, you'd think she was absolutely desolated by her stepdaughter's death. Which was it? Maybe a little bit of both? Lucy thought of her own girls and how difficult she sometimes found them. That didn't mean she didn't love Elizabeth, Sara, and Zoe, she did. It was just that sometimes she found their behavior so exasperating that she wanted to strangle them — but restrained herself. Unlike Lily, who was a stepmother, she was her daughters' biological mother. She'd carried them in her body, beneath her heart, and labored to bring them into the world. She'd nursed them and potty-trained them, watched them learn to talk and walk. They were part of her in a way that Taylor and Parker were not part of Lily.

And the girls were only about ten years younger than Lily, which was weird, and which brought in the whole question of the three women's various relationships with Scott. Had Lily replaced the girls in Scott's heart? Were they rivals for his attention? Did she see them as spoiled Daddy's girls? Did they see her as a gold digger? Were they resentful, believing that she had replaced their mother? Who was their mother, anyway, and how did she figure in this family drama?

Lucy suddenly realized that she'd been scrubbing the same dish for so long that she was in danger of erasing the floral transferware pattern printed on it, and rinsed it off, setting it in the drainer. That chore done, she found herself yawning, and decided to head upstairs for a little nap. It had been quite a day, including that lively game of soccer, and she was exhausted.

The staircase seemed steeper and taller than it had previously when she hauled herself up to the second floor. There she retreated to her room, where she laid down on top of the quilted bedspread, covering herself by pulling up the hand-crocheted afghan that was folded at the foot of the bed. She picked up one of the books thoughtfully provided for her on the nightstand, but only managed to read a paragraph or two of Sarah Orne Jewett's prose before the book dropped from her hand and she fell asleep.

It was not a peaceful sleep, however, as she tossed and turned, flinging off the afghan when she grew too warm. Her mind was filled with surreal and distorted images of gulls wheeling overhead, waves crashing relentlessly on the rocky shore, and Parker falling through thin air. Then a flashback, but it wasn't Parker, it was Zoe and she was struggling with Mike. They were standing on the edge of a precipice, above a bottomless pit, and she was running toward them, trying to warn them of the danger. They didn't see or hear her; they began arguing and Mike grabbed Zoe by the shoulders and gave a shove, sending Zoe over the edge. Lucy reached the edge and saw her daughter floating slowly downward, getting smaller and smaller until she was a little dot swallowed up by blackness.

Suddenly startled awake by a loud gong, Lucy tried to erase the image from her mind. It was only a dream, she told herself, a crazy jumble combining her fears for her daughter with the tragic situation on the island. A second clang of the gong called her to her senses and she realized it was dinnertime. She hauled herself out of the tangled afghan and straightened her clothes, then stopped at the bathroom for a quick pee and wash up. She splashed a little cold water on her face and patted it dry with a towel, staring for a moment at her reflection in the mirror over the sink. She looked the same as always, which didn't seem right since everything had changed. She wasn't the same person who had arrived at the island yesterday expecting a welcome change from her everyday routine; now she didn't know what she was doing here and more than anything, she wanted to leave. She didn't want to be involved in the Newman family's tragic drama, but she had no choice. There was no way off the island until the ferry came. She was stuck and had to make the best of it.

So she went downstairs and into the dining room, where there was an extra place set at the table. Was it some sort of tribute to the missing daughter, or was it a simple mistake? It was certainly awkward, everyone was eyeing it but not saying anything.

Susan came in with a tureen and, noticing the unoccupied chair, quickly set the tureen down and apologized. "Oh, my goodness, what was I thinking?" she exclaimed, gathering up the unneeded plate and silverware. "I'm so sorry," she added.

"A natural mistake, I'm sure," said Lily, standing up and beginning to ladle out servings of lobster bisque.

Scott didn't say anything, but reached for his glass of whiskey and took a sip. Lucy suspected he'd been sipping all day long, but couldn't find it in her heart to blame him.

Susan returned with a bowl of salad and a basket of warm rolls. "Here you go," she said, setting them down. "I didn't think you'd want a big, heavy meal, but there's more of that lobster bisque in the kitchen if you want it."

"Thank you, Susan," said Lily. "The bisque looks delicious."

Susan slipped away into the kitchen, and Lily finished serving the lobster bisque. Lucy found it absolutely delicious, but noticed that Lily and Taylor barely tasted it. Scott didn't touch his at all, but picked at a roll and drank his whiskey, eventually getting up to refill his glass. The boys ate heartily, but there was still plenty of bisque left in the tureen when Susan came to clear the table. "Anyone for dessert?" she asked. "There was still some of the ice cream from the party left in the icehouse and it ought to be eaten up, it won't keep for long in the ice box." She was thoughtful. "I salvaged everything I could from the icehouse before they put the body in, it's not sanitary, if you know what I mean. . . ."

They all knew what she meant. Lily let out a sob and ran from the room; they could hear her running up the stairs. Scott refilled his glass for the second time, then left the dining room, taking it with him. That left Lucy at the table with Taylor and the twins, and Susan, who stood waiting for a decision about dessert.

"I guess we'll all have some ice cream," said Taylor, speaking in a tight, little voice. "It would be a shame to waste it after you went to so much trouble to make it."

When the bowls of ice cream arrived, covered with chocolate sauce, the boys dove right in. Taylor and Lucy ate more slowly, in silence, as if consuming the ice cream was taking part in some sort of ritual. Finally, Taylor spoke. "I was wondering if you'd like to help me with the puffin project, Lucy." She sighed, taking a moment to master her emotions. "It's really too much for me, without Parker."

Lucy's spirits immediately lifted; here was something she could do that was positively helpful. "I'd love to," she said. "When do we start?"

"Well, it's best to get going before dawn, because the parents return in the morning to feed the chicks. They spend the night at sea. Is that going to be a problem?"

"Nope, I'm an early riser," said Lucy. She turned to the boys. "How about a game of Monopoly? I'm pretty sure I can beat you

117

this time."

Fred leveled his eyes at her. "I wouldn't be too confident if I were you."

She stared right back at him, thinking that although the twins seemed to be as identical as two peas in a pod, they were really quite different. Fred was a bit of a schemer, and not afraid of a confrontation, while Walter was more of a good-time guy, eager to please.

"Oh, yeah," she finally replied. "You're the one who should be worried."

But as she shepherded the boys into the living room, she knew she was just putting up a brave front. She was worried, and not about losing the game.

CHAPTER SEVEN

The jangle of the old-fashioned windup alarm clock woke Lucy out of a deep sleep at what seemed to be the middle of the night but was only, if the clock was to be believed, four thirty. She made her way down the dark hallway to the bathroom and splashed cold water on her face, then went back to her room, where she resisted the temptation to crawl back between the covers. Instead, she dressed warmly in jeans and a long-sleeved sweatshirt over a short-sleeved tee. That way she was ready whether the sun burned off the morning chill or not, which she decided was more likely. She decided to take her waterproof windbreaker, too, in case of rain. Who'd've thunk it, she marveled, that she'd actually miss the morning weather forecast on the TV news, but it was darned inconvenient to start the day without it.

She crept downstairs to the kitchen, where

Taylor was filling a thermos with coffee. "You made it!" she said, speaking softly. "I was wondering if you'd really get up so early."

"I was sorely tempted to go back to bed," admitted Lucy, "and my body is not convinced it's really awake. Any chance of a cup of coffee before we go?"

"Oh, sure," said Taylor, filling a mug for her. "And you ought to eat something. Susan usually leaves muffins for us early birds." She went into the pantry and returned with a tin that she set on the table and opened, revealing a loaf of date-nut bread. She quickly slapped the cover back on and sat down, covering her eyes with her hand. "Parker's favorite," she said.

Lucy wasn't sure what to do. She was hungry and desperately wanted some breakfast, but she didn't want to desecrate the memorial loaf, either.

"I'm sorry," said Taylor, quickly brushing away the tears with her hand. "That just came at me out of left base, if you know what I mean." She stood up and got a knife out of the drawer. "Parker wouldn't want us to waste it."

"Of course not," said Lucy, accepting a thick slab of date-nut bread with a generous slathering of butter for breakfast. Taylor also cut herself a piece, but only nibbled at it before announcing it was time to get moving.

The sky was lightening when they started out, and the wind had died down, leaving the island covered with fog. The fog was so thick that they could see only a few feet ahead and they paused on the porch to don their waterproof jackets. Crossing the lawn was like walking through a cloud, thought Lucy, feeling the moist air on her face and hands. Visibility was somewhat better in the woods, and they had little difficulty following the path, but when they emerged at the nesting ground the fog was once again quite thick. She couldn't see the ocean, but she could hear the waves pounding against the rocks below.

"You need to be very careful," warned Taylor. "You don't want to fall off the cliff."

"Do you think that's what happened to Parker?" asked Lucy, immediately regretting the question. "Oh, I'm so sorry. . . ."

"It wasn't foggy that night," said Taylor, in a matter-of-fact tone that made Lucy wonder if she'd been thinking the same thing. "There was almost a full moon. I think she must have had a dizzy spell or something."

"Why do you think she was out here at

night?" asked Lucy.

"She might have been worried about a predator; there were signs something had been trying to get at the chicks."

"What signs?" asked Lucy.

"Oh, disturbed earth, that sort of thing," said Taylor.

Curious, Lucy looked around but didn't see any disturbed earth. Of course, she admitted to herself, she was unfamiliar with the area and might not recognize a damaged nesting burrow even if it was right in front of her. "Right," she said. "So what do we do?"

"Okay." Taylor produced a couple of clipboards that contained a few sheets of paper beneath a protective sheet of clear plastic and handed one to Lucy. "This sheet is a grid that matches the nesting area. Do you see?"

Lucy looked and immediately made out the plan, noting the irregular coastline and various features such as boulders and a scraggly, misshapen pine tree. The location of each nesting burrow was marked with a numbered X. "I do."

"The chicks have hatched. The eggs were laid sometime in May, and incubation takes about five or six weeks. Once hatched they stay in their nest burrows and are fed by both parents, who bring them sand eels and other goodies. The parents fly out to sea in the evening, when there's less chance of predation, and they actually roost and sleep at sea. In the morning they do some fishing and feeding, and then they fly home with breakfast for the kids. The challenge for us is to check on the chick's progress before Mom and Dad come home, because they will dive-bomb us and, if they get a chance, give us a nasty bite."

"Wow. I had no idea they could be so aggressive. Puffins are cute, like little clownish penguins with those black and white suits and bright orange beaks and feet. I sent a stuffed one to my grandson for Christmas one year, along with a storybook."

"Truth is stranger than fiction," said Taylor, with a little laugh. "They're busy little excavators, too, so you have to be careful where you step or you could break an ankle. Keep checking the grid and remember that the ground around each burrow can be quite unstable."

"Okay," said Lucy, beginning to think she'd taken on rather more than she expected. "So how exactly do we check the burrows?"

"Well," said Taylor, breaking into a big smile, "you've got to kind of crawl until you reach the opening and then you shove your hand inside and grab the chick. Pull him out and look him over, assessing his condition. There's a chart for each chick, same number as the burrow, and you check off his condition and guesstimate his growth. See?"

She flipped through the papers on the clipboard and showed Lucy one of the charts. "See, you check off whether the little guy is vigorous or not. Parasites? Well-fed? Flapping wings? It's pretty straightforward. Okay?"

"Okay."

"So I'll start on the left side, you take the right, and we'll meet in the middle."

Mindful of Taylor's instructions, Lucy made her way carefully to the edge of the nesting area and, following Taylor's movements, dropped to her knees and began crawling to the first burrow on her chart. She'd never liked sticking her hand into dark spaces, like the nasty and spidery kitchen cabinets she'd cleared out for Bill in some of his restoration projects, so she steeled herself before shoving her arm into that first burrow. There were no spiders, no snakes, just a warm, little, feathery creature she was easily able to grasp gently. She pulled it out and examined it, noting the little fellow's downy feathers and bright eyes. Comparing the bird in her hand with the one pictured on the chart, she noted it was larger and heavier and was beginning to flap its immature wings. Unlike its parents, the chick was a study in white and gray with no orange feet or beak. It wasn't all that pleased at being handled, however, and attempted to nip her hand with its beak.

"Okay, little one, back you go." She set the chick down in the burrow opening and watched as it disappeared into the tunnel and the comfort and security of the nesting chamber.

Moving on to the next burrow, she noticed that Taylor was making faster progress than she was, and realized she'd have to work at a faster pace. The sun was up, revealed as a bright spot in the fog, and she knew the adults would soon be returning to feed their chicks. She was muscle sore, sweaty, and her face and hands were scratched from the brushy undergrowth when she met Taylor, not at the middle but having covered about a third of the charted area. A few of the birds had already arrived, so they pulled on hoods and ducked as low as they could, hurrying back to the cover of the pinewoods.

Once they reached safety, they stripped off their jackets and unzipped their sweatshirts. It was still cool, too cool for T-shirts, but they had both worked up a sweat from crawling around in the stiff, waterproof jackets that protected them from the brush and the aggressive birds. "Thanks, Lucy," said Taylor, breathing heavily. "I couldn't have done it without you, and if we don't keep up with the schedule, everything we've done so far becomes useless." She paused. "I didn't want that to happen."

"When does it end?" asked Lucy, wondering what Taylor would do once she left the island.

"In about three weeks the chicks will fly off. They'll leave in the night and won't be seen again until they return to the island as adults to breed."

"Where do they go?" asked Lucy, horrified at this apparent lack of family feeling.

"To sea. They're seabirds. They just bob about on the water; they sleep, eat, do everything except mate out at sea. They keep to themselves except when they're breeding."

"All alone in the big ocean?" The idea bothered Lucy. This wasn't how she thought puffins ought to behave. Shouldn't they stick together?

"Yeah." Taylor nodded and smiled, amused by Lucy's reaction.

Another thought occurred to Lucy as they started back through the woods. "What about the cliff face? Do some of the puffins nest there?"

"Oh, sure. The experienced birds return to their old burrows; the scientists aren't sure if the birds actually mate for life or if they're primarily attracted to the burrow, returning year after year. There's a lot of competition for vacant burrows, like for affordable apartments in New York. The younger birds have to make do with whatever they can find." She paused, apparently reading Lucy's mind. "It's way too dangerous for us to check them, and Parker wouldn't have tried." She paused. "And certainly not at night, in the dark."

Lucy agreed, having experienced the terrain firsthand. It was dangerous, even treacherous, and she couldn't imagine what Parker was doing there at night. But she must have been. The question was why, why did she go and what was she doing? "There must have been a reason," said Lucy. "I didn't see any signs of predation, did you?"

"She did say something about it the other night, but maybe it was a cover, in case she got caught going out," said Taylor. "She might have been meeting someone."

"One of the guys?"

"Obviously," said Taylor in a rather sarcastic tone.

"Right, so who was it? Will?"

Taylor looked surprised. "Will?" She shrugged. "Maybe. I don't know. She played her cards close to her chest when it came to guys."

As the mother of three girls, Lucy understood why Parker might not have wanted to admit her interest in a particular guy for fear that her sister might attempt to steal him. Sara and Zoe were jealous of each other, and had been known to fight over each other's boyfriends. They were quite different physically, however, unlike the identical twins Parker and Taylor, who were presumably equally attractive. If a guy was drawn to one of the twins because of her appearance, he'd probably like the other one, too.

"My daughters are private like that, too," said Lucy. "But you must have had an inkling, right?"

"Not really." She paused, then sighed. "I know I shouldn't speak ill of the dead, and we're not supposed to get into slut shaming, but the truth is that Parker was really rather promiscuous. She was probably planning to have a little fling with each of the guys before the summer was over, kind of a sexy smorgasbord."

"More power to her," said Lucy, somewhat shocked but determined not to show it. She couldn't imagine Sara or Zoe behaving like that.

"Oh, she liked girls, too," added Taylor. "No one was safe."

"That kind of behavior can be dangerous," said Lucy.

"You think?" They had reached the end of the trail through the woods and Taylor broke away, hurrying across an open field in the direction of the farm. Lucy headed in the other direction, walking slowly toward the house. She didn't go right inside when she reached the porch, but sat on one of the wicker chairs to rest and take in the view. The fog had cleared somewhat and she could make out the shadowy form of the gazebo, but the sea beyond remained invisible. After a bit she got up and was turning to go into the house when she noticed Taylor emerging from the perimeter trail, along with Brad, and saw the two walking together until they entered the gazebo. Lucy knew it was certainly not the sort of day for swimming, it would be foolhardy to venture out on the rocks in such dense fog. The changing rooms in the lower level of the gazebo did offer privacy, however, and she figured that was their likely destination.

They didn't have to be going there for sex, there were a million reasons why two people might want to be together. Maybe they liked to do jigsaw puzzles, or were writing a song together, or penning a letter to their congressman. It was just that Taylor had been talking about her sexy sister, which made Lucy wonder if Parker was more like Taylor in that respect than she let on. Lucy suddenly felt old as she climbed the stairs, and hopelessly old-fashioned. This was a strange new world where babies were conceived in test tubes and things that were once forbidden were now accepted. It was probably progress, she conceded, but she needed a little time to adjust to the new standards.

Plopping herself down on her bed and untying her hiking shoes, she wondered if perhaps the proverb that said the more things changed, the more they stayed the same, was still true. What was the relationship between Brad and Taylor, and how did it affect Parker, if at all? It was the first lead she'd had and she decided to follow it. But first, she wanted a late breakfast.

Back downstairs, she headed for the kitchen, where she found Susan busy washing lettuce.

"That's a real chore," said Lucy. "Fresh

lettuce tastes great, but it's a lot of work."

"I don't mind," said Susan. "The water's cool and the leaves feel silky and look so pretty. What I don't like is messing with this old woodstove. It's a beast and I'm just beginning to get the hang of the thing."

"How do you cook at your place, without electricity?"

"I use propane. Scott doesn't like it, but I told him it was non-negotiable. We have to eat, too. I've got three men to feed at home and there's not enough time in the day for me to work here all day and then try to whip up a quick meal on a woodstove."

"Aha, so there is room for negotiation," said Lucy. "Any chance I can negotiate a late breakfast?"

"There's still some oatmeal on the back of the stove," said Susan. "Help yourself."

Lucy found a generous helping in the simmering double boiler and scooped it into a blue and white transferware bowl, then added sugar and milk. "Thanks," she said, after popping a spoonful into her mouth and savoring the nutty flavor. "This is delicious."

"I have to admit the woodstove is great for oatmeal. I mix it up the night before and it cooks slowly all night on the banked stove. You can't beat it."

As she ate, Lucy thought about Susan's insistence on having a modern propane stove, and wondered if she'd forced Scott to make any other concessions. "You know," she began, "I can't quite believe that there is really no way to communicate from the island. Even if Scott wants to go back to the middle of the nineteenth century, it wouldn't hurt to have a marine radio tucked away somewhere, just in case of an emergency. You guys could have one, couldn't you? I mean, how would he know?"

"He'd know if the state police and the medical examiner suddenly showed up," muttered Susan. She quickly added, "Not that we've got such a thing, but if we did, it would be risky to use it."

"I suppose it would," said Lucy, polishing off the last of the oatmeal.

Susan had finished washing the lettuce and was wrapping it in clean dish towels to dry, so Lucy took her bowl and the empty pot to the sink and began washing them. The bowl cleaned up easily, but the top of the double boiler presented a challenge as it was coated with solidified oatmeal. She tried scrubbing, but without a modern scrubbing pad and only the quaint dishmop at hand she found it tough going.

"You'll have to soak it," advised Susan

with a smile. "I put in a bit of baking soda and it usually comes off just in time to start the new batch."

"Okay," said Lucy, picking up the yellow box of baking soda that Susan kept on the windowsill above the sink. "So you really think Scott would be furious if you radioed for help?"

"He won't let me have a non-scratch nylon scrub pad," said Susan. "What do you think?"

"I think baking soda works wonders," said Lucy.

"It can't do everything," muttered Susan, picking up one of the trugs that were stacked by the door and heading out to the garden.

Lucy left the pot to soak and wandered into the living room, not quite sure what to do with herself. The room was empty so she picked up an old *Town & Country* magazine and flipped through the pages advertising jewelry that was so expensive one had to call for the price — and probably submit to a few questions about one's net worth before getting an answer. She tossed the magazine aside and reached for a *National Geographic,* but didn't open it. Instead, she thought about her conversation with Susan, who had practically admitted that she had access to a marine radio but was hesitant to use it because it would anger Scott.

That was simply crazy, she decided. What if Parker hadn't died in the fall, but needed medical care? Would he allow the use of the radio then? It was one thing to try to simplify one's life and to choose to do without modern conveniences, but there were limits. She thought of court cases against parents who refused to allow lifesaving medical treatment for a child stricken with cancer because of their beliefs. You could sympathize up to a point, but in the end she believed it was the child's life that mattered.

Lucy had been to historic re-creations, where actors portrayed people who had lived hundreds of years earlier, and she'd even covered mock battles, re-creating encounters between the early colonists and the British. They made great photos and stories for the paper, and were educational, too. But those people took off their nineteenth-century costumes at the end of the day and went home to microwave popcorn and TV shows.

There was something more going on with Scott, she decided, than a desire to simplify his life. There was a reason he insisted on staying off the grid, and she suspected it did not have anything to do with historical accuracy or saving the environment. It was more likely that the man was suffering from delusions and paranoia, including the not entirely unfounded fear that the World Wide Web was a two-way street inviting observation by others. She herself had stuck a little, round Band-Aid on the camera eye atop her computer screen, though she was not entirely sure it was necessary. Of course, Scott was a rich and powerful man, and had more to fear from those who might wish to do him harm. It was those fears, she believed, that were clouding his judgment and causing him to engage in bizarre, controlling behavior. That was the only explanation that made sense, and Lucy didn't like it. Here she was, stuck on an island, at the mercy of a man who she suspected was losing his sanity.

CHAPTER EIGHT

There was no point in confronting Scott, the very idea made her nervous, especially after talking with Susan. Not only was the man struggling with his inner demons, he now had the added burden of grieving for his daughter, not to mention his precious Watson yacht. There was no telling how he might react if pressed, and Lucy wasn't about to find out. No, she thought, her best option was to find one of the Hopkins men. They had been living on the island long before Scott appeared and no doubt had forged ties with other fishermen and mainlanders. She knew a bit about hardy, and some said stubborn and contrary, native Mainers who had developed skills that enabled them to cope with an unforgiving and hostile environment, and she figured the Hopkinses were prime examples of the breed. Scott might think he was running things on the island, but she suspected that was only an illusion the Hopkins family allowed him to maintain, as long as they gained some advantages from the deception.

She was feeling restless, anyway, so she decided to go out for a walk and explore part of the island she hadn't seen yet. If she happened to encounter one of the Hopkins men, well, it would only be polite to engage in conversation. So she went outside and walked around the house and instead of taking the perimeter trail, chose the path that led past the flower garden and through the field, toward the farm.

This path was much more open than the one that led to the puffins' nesting area, running through tall meadow grass and wildflowers rather than through pinewoods. It meandered a bit, curving round a few large boulders, but it wasn't long before she heard a male voice singing a sea chantey. At first she thought it was simply a bit of icing on the cake, a tongue-in-cheek bit of acting on the part of an old-time seafaring character, but then she remembered how her husband liked to play a radio while he worked. "It makes the time go faster, gives you a bit of a rhythm to work by," he once told her. The Hopkinses couldn't have a radio, so she figured they did the next best thing and revived some old-time chanteys they'd probably heard as kids.

Finally stepping into the cleared area around that huge barn, she discovered the singer was Hopp, the family patriarch, who was seated in front of a shed, repairing wire lobster traps. He didn't notice her, so she yelled out a hello and waited for an invitation to visit.

"Ahoy!" called out Hopp, giving her a smile. "What brings you here?" The little fuzz of fluffy white hair on his mostly bald head and his worn, paint-stained chinos reminded her of her grandfather, who had always been busy with some project or other.

"Just exploring," said Lucy, crossing the hard-packed soil where a few tufts of grass sprouted. "I didn't like being cooped up in the house."

"Understandable," said Hopp, deftly wielding a pair of pliers. "After all, it's a house of grief. It must be awkward for you."

"You said it," agreed Lucy, impressed by Hopp's sensitivity. "I've been trying to help out as much as I can, but there's not much to do right now. They've all retreated to their rooms as far as I can tell."

"Even the boys?" asked Hopp, looking puzzled.

"No sign of them."

"Hmmm." Hopp put down his pliers. "That's not good. 'Course this weather isn't helping. I'd take 'em out fishing, but not in this fog. Too dangerous."

"Does fog like this happen often?" asked Lucy.

Hopp shrugged. "Now and then."

"Does it usually last very long?"

"Depends."

A typical Maine answer if she'd ever heard one, thought Lucy. "Will the ferry be able to come?"

"Oh, yeah. They've got radar, sonar, all that modern technology that Newman hates. And the captain's done it for years; Pete Peterson knows his way around these islands." He paused. "You can tell time by the state ferry."

"And what then?" asked Lucy. "Will the Newmans leave the island? Will they send the body? Will there be an investigation? And what about the boats?"

"Your guess is as good as mine," he replied. "The death has to be reported, and the medical examiner will want to see the body before issuing a death certificate. I imagine Scott will accompany the body, but I'm just guessing."

"Is that what usually happens when there's

a death on the island?"

Hopp took a moment before answering. "You know, it's been a long time since anyone died. The last was my grandpa, some ten years ago. There was a doctor on the island then, a retired fella, and he issued the death certificate. We buried him here. Gramps wouldn't've wanted it any other way." He paused, exchanging one set of pliers for another. "It's all changed now, I imagine Cap'n Pete will know what's required."

"And Scott will have to give up his illusions," said Lucy.

"It's not going to be easy for him," said Hopp with a sly smile. "He thinks he's the king of the Quahog Republic."

"I don't think republics have kings," said Lucy, watching as Hopp set aside the trap he had been working on and reached for another. "And are you sure it's okay with Scott for you to use wire traps, instead of the old-style wooden ones?"

"You can't find the wood ones anymore," said Hopp, grinning and revealing a few missing teeth. "All gone for coffee tables, that's why."

Lucy laughed. She'd seen plenty of lobster trap coffee tables for sale in souvenir shops and sometimes set out for sale on people's lawns, along with brightly painted home-made whirligigs and striped miniature lighthouses. "I'm surprised you've got time to mend lobster traps, what with having to keep the boat in Tinker's Cove and all you've got to do here on the island."

"We're selling the boat," said Hopp. "And the traps, too. I'm just getting 'em cleaned up and ready to go."

"Too much trouble, since you can't keep it here, on the island?" asked Lucy.

"Yup, not enough hours in the day, what with sailing over to the Cove and all. The boys tried staying over there, in town, but we need 'em here on the island. It was too much for me to do alone, taking care of the gardening and the farm all by myself."

"What do Wolf and Ben do?" asked Lucy.

"Good question," said Hopp. He shrugged. "I really shouldn't say that. They cut firewood, they fetch and carry, they mow the grass and pull the weeds, they keep the boats shipshape. . . ."

"They didn't do such a good job, did they?"

"Mebbe." Hopp shrugged. "That's the thing with living on an island, you know. There's not a lot of room for error. Main-landers don't quite get it."

"But you and your family have stayed

here, right? For hundreds of years even?"

"Yup, that old graveyard is full of Hopkinses, and plenty others, too. Used to be a lot of folk on this island."

"They left, but you stayed, right?"

"We was actually thinking of leaving a few years ago, but the Island Institute offered us a chance to participate in a wind-power project. We wouldn't've had to put up any cash; they were gonna erect the turbines and all. It would've made a big difference out here. We figured it might well bring some folks who'd left back to the island."

"What happened?" asked Lucy.

"Newman, that's what happened. He bought the island. . . ."

"From you?"

"Nah, the bank. We had one of those balloon mortgages and it came due and we couldn't pay. We asked for an extension, always got one before, but the old local bank was bought out by one o' those big national banks and Scott waved cash in front of their greedy eyes and that's what happened. And then he turned around and gave it to that darn Land Trust, and they put an end to any idea of wind turbines. Too dangerous for the birds, they said, but I think if a bird's too dumb to avoid a wind turbine, it's pretty much too dumb to survive." He snorted.

"Seems those puffins are more important than people, at least to some people."

"Well, I guess they're endangered."

"Not endangered. Only threatened." He smacked his lips. "Ever eat puffin?"

"Can't say I have," admitted Lucy. "Are they good?"

"Can be. My mother used to do them real nice, but that's in the past. We don't eat 'em anymore. Times change."

Lucy sensed a tone of regret in Hopp's voice, and she wondered why the family had stayed on the island after Scott bought it.

"I imagine a lot of things have changed on the island, thanks to Scott," said Lucy. "He's taken you all back to the middle of the nineteenth century. How do you feel about that?"

"He can't keep it up, you can't stop progress. I imagine he's learning that lesson right now."

"I'm not so sure," said Lucy. "If anything, I'd say that losing Parker has just made him dig his heels in harder. And now that the boats are gone, especially that yacht of his, it's reinforcing his fears." She chewed her lip. "Sometimes I worry about his sanity."

Hopp shrugged. "Takes all kinds, that's what my mother used to say, and you shouldn't judge people 'til you've walked a

143

mile in their shoes. She was pretty sharp, and the older I get the more I realize it. She also used to say that people come, people go, but there's always been Hopkinses on this island. It's our island, always has been, always will be." He set aside the trap he was working on and slapped his hands on his thighs, then stood up. "Well, it's time I was getting on."

Lucy took the hint. "It's been nice talking to you, but I guess I better get back."

"Watch out for that redtail," he warned. "She's got a nest and she's not shy about guarding it."

"I'll be careful," said Lucy, figuring the warning was a joke, or maybe a way of telling her to stay away from the wooded part of the island. She gave him a wave as she headed back toward the path. She walked slowly, not at all eager to get back to the oppressive atmosphere in the house, and let her mind wander, much as the meandering path wandered through the meadow. She thought about Hopp's parting words, his assertion that the island had always belonged to the Hopkinses and always would. For a moment she wondered if Hopp had some sort of evil plan to eliminate the Newman family one by one, but realized that would be futile.

It was once true, she thought, that the Hopkinses owned the island, but now it belonged to the trust, and the Hopkinses and Newmans only had occupancy rights during Scott Newman's lifetime. When Scott died, the island would no longer be inhabited by humans and would revert to its natural state as a home for puffins and other wildlife. There would be no point in eliminating the interlopers because there was no way the Hopkins family could remain on the island; she had written about the Maine Coast Land Trust for the *Pennysaver* and knew that the organization knew the law inside and out, and made sure there were no loopholes in its contracts. Once a piece of property was deeded to the trust, it stayed with the trust. Legally binding meant exactly that, no exclusions.

Hopp was probably just blowing off steam, repeating a family mantra that he wished were still true. Maybe it was simply a bit of magical thinking, she thought, aware that sometimes she did the same thing. Maybe Zoe would tire of that awful Mike Snider, for example. Maybe Bill would suggest going out for dinner and a movie some night as a surprise. Maybe the fog would clear and the ferry boat would come early.

By now she was through the field and on

the green grass of the lawn that encircled the mansion with its generous porches and tall tower, but she wasn't ready to go back inside. Instead, she decided to give herself some time to overcome her reluctance and sat herself down on a rustic, twig bench that overlooked the lawn. She stared at the house, recalling her first sight of it. Then it had seemed to signify everything that she aspired to: an abundant life of ease and grace in a beautiful, tastefully restored old house. She'd been impressed by Scott Newman's wealth and generosity, and his commitment to the environment. She remembered the night of the party, when there'd been music and laughter; Lily had even sung for everyone, and Parker and Taylor had charmed everyone with their beauty and eagerness to please. She remembered how the Newman family had entranced her that evening and how eager she'd been to return to the island.

That first night back there'd been a wonderful family dinner around the big table in the dining room, followed by board games. It had reminded her of her own family, and how they, too, used to play after-supper games of Monopoly and Trivial Pursuit. But that had been a long time ago, when the kids were still little. As they grew older, they lost interest in family games. She couldn't imagine getting Zoe or Sara to play now, not even to amuse their little nephew Patrick. Suddenly she wondered if the Newmans had been putting on a show of family togetherness for her benefit. Or for their own? Because it now seemed, after Parker's death, that there was very little holding them together.

After the games ended and the boys were sent to bed, Lucy remembered how Scott had withdrawn to the porch as the evening grew darker and night fell. He liked to gaze at the stars, Lily had said, and when Lucy went up to bed she had opened the window and looked out, amazed by the huge number of stars, which she'd never seen so clearly, or so brightly. She'd been enthralled, and she remembered hearing laughter in the distance. Who was it, she wondered, laughing out there in the night? Was Parker out there with Will? And had he, or maybe one of the other young men on the island, lured her out to the back of the island to see the rising moon? And had there been some sort of altercation, or even a playful tussle, that ended with her falling over the edge of the cliff?

She shivered, sitting there on the bench, and suddenly stood up, striding energetically across the lawn. It didn't bear thinking about, she decided. Parker's death was an accident, a tragic accident. How could it be anything else? Under those stars, in that magical night, in this beautiful place, murder simply wasn't possible.

CHAPTER NINE

The boys were on the porch, putting together a big floor puzzle of a T. rex dinosaur, and Lucy paused to greet them. "I think that big brown piece goes under his chin," she suggested.

"Nope, it's part of his tail," said Fred, snapping the piece into place.

"We've done this puzzle a million times," said Walter, adding a big sigh. "It's no fun."

"There's nothing to do, and we're not supposed to make any noise that would disturb Mom," explained Fred.

"Maybe you should try a harder puzzle," suggested Lucy.

"This one's for babies," complained Walter, slapping in the pieces one by one, "but the others are all too hard. They've got thousands of pieces."

Lucy sympathized with the boys' plight and decided they could use a little adult attention. "Well, I know a good game: Twenty

Questions. You think of something and tell me if it's animal, vegetable, or mineral. Then I've got twenty chances to ask questions and figure out what it is. Want to play?"

The two looked at each other, and grinned. Then put their heads together and whispered, finally coming to an agreement. "We've got it. It's animal," said Fred.

"Is it feathered?" asked Lucy, spotting a sea gull flying overhead.

"Yes," said Fred.

"No," said Walter.

"Of course, it's got feathers," insisted Fred.

"Not yet it doesn't," said Walter.

"It's an egg, right?" said Lucy.

"Aw, she got it," moaned Fred. " 'Cause of you."

"Me? 'Cause of you!" exclaimed Walter, attempting to grab his twin.

Fred eluded his brother's grasp and started running across the lawn, only to be pursued by Walter. Lucy got to her feet and watched the chase, concluding that the game was over. They were acting like brothers again, which she thought was a hopeful sign. The clock in the hall was chiming six o'clock when she went in, which meant dinner would be in half an hour. She went upstairs to wash up, deciding to change into warmer clothes for the evening. It wasn't just the possibility of cooler temperatures that motivated her, she wasn't quite comfortable about presenting herself to the grief-stricken family in shorts and T-shirt. In her room she chose a pair of khaki slacks and a long-sleeved navy polo shirt, tossing a cotton sweater over her shoulders and tying the sleeves. Preppy casual, for sure, but more suitable for the present situation.

She encountered Taylor in the upstairs hallway and was reassured when she saw she was wearing a similar outfit, although Taylor's shirt sported a designer logo, and she was wearing a gold chain necklace, little gold hoop earrings, and a sporty Rolex watch. Together they went downstairs, Lucy feeling like the budget version of an expensive look in a magazine: one hundred dollars for this outfit versus thousands for the designer original.

Lucy's sense of not belonging, of being an outsider, grew stronger when they gathered at the table. Scott had been drinking before dinner and continued during the meal, refilling his glass with whiskey several times. He was largely silent, rousing himself occasionally to comment gruffly on the boys' behavior, urging them to clean their plates because Susan had gone to a lot of trouble to prepare the baked beans and brown bread dinner.

Lily, still wearing that fluttery white chiffon top and skinny black pants, had retouched her makeup and hair, which was now smoothly tucked into a black headband. She pointedly ignored Scott, focusing her attention instead on the twin boys.

"Clean plate club members get pie for dessert," she told them, offering a carrot instead of Scott's stick.

"What kind?" asked Fred.

"I think it's strawberry-rhubarb," admitted Lily.

"Ugh," moaned Walter. "That's yucky."

"Well, eat up anyway. You'll need energy tomorrow," advised Lily.

"What are we going to do tomorrow?" asked Fred. "It's the Fourth of July, right? Are there going to be fireworks?"

"I don't think so," said Lily, looking at Scott for confirmation and getting a shake of the head.

"No fireworks!" exclaimed Fred. "That stinks."

"Yeah," added Walter. "We've gotta have fireworks."

"It wouldn't be proper, it would be disrespectful to Parker," said Lily.

"Parker loved fireworks, she'd want us to

have them," said Fred.

"What are we gonna do if we don't have fireworks? It's supposed to be a holiday," argued Walter.

"Oh, I don't know. More of what you did today, I suppose."

"Boring," said Fred. "I wish we had TV."

"That's enough! You've got a whole island!" roared Scott, thumping his fist on the table and making the plates and silverware jump. The ice tinkled in his glass.

"Maybe you'd like to see the puffins," suggested Taylor.

Lucy was surprised by Taylor's offer, since she hadn't shown much interest in the boys. But maybe she was trying to keep busy as a way of managing her grief.

"Lucy helped me today and she had a great time," continued Taylor. "Isn't that right, Lucy?"

"They're so interesting," said Lucy, taking the hint and doing her part to keep the conversation going. "Do you know that after they've had their chicks they go to sea, all by themselves? Those little birds spend most of their lives all alone, bobbing around on the ocean. Can you imagine?"

Walter looked concerned. "What about the chicks? Do they go, too?"

"They do," said Taylor. "When they're

ready they just fly off in the night, because that's when it's safest, and they stay out at sea until they're ready to come back to the island and breed."

"What do they eat?" asked Fred, spreading butter on his brown bread.

"Fish."

"I'm glad I'm not a puffin," said Walter.

"Sounds awful," offered Fred, "but better than being stuck here. I wouldn't mind being by myself, anywhere but here."

"Oh, you say that but you wouldn't really like it," said Lily, jumping in to avoid further negativity from Scott. "We're a family, we stick together. We love each other."

Her effort wasn't entirely successful. "Let it go," grumbled Scott. "It's no good." He heaved himself out of his chair and stumbled off into the living room from where they heard a solid thud.

"Will he be all right?" asked Lucy, ready to follow him and make sure he had landed on a sofa to sleep it off.

"He'll be fine," said Lily, placidly. "Who'd like some pie?"

Everybody did, even the boys, when they learned it wasn't strawberry-rhubarb after all, but lemon meringue instead.

Afterward, in the kitchen, Lucy asked Susan where she got fresh lemons.

"Weren't fresh," confessed Susan. "I used juice from a bottle."

It was cozy in the old-fashioned kitchen, where the oil lamps that supplemented the single bare lightbulb that dangled from a cord on the ceiling gave a feeling of intimacy that Lucy hoped might encourage Susan to share more information about the islanders.

"It was awfully good," said Lucy, scraping the plates into a bucket of leftover scraps that would eventually go to feed the chickens. "The boys loved it."

"I wish this fog would clear — we could sure use some fresh fish," said Susan.

"Hopp was saying that, too," said Lucy. "I saw him today and he said he wished he could take the boys out and give them something to do." She added the plate to the stack of dirty dishes on the counter next to the sink. "So I guess you've got a boat?"

"Just a wheelbarrow dory, nothing big enough to get to the mainland, if that's what you was thinking," said Susan, filling the sink with sudsy water.

"Scott seems to be taking Parker's death very hard," observed Lucy, grabbing a dish towel and preparing to dry while Susan washed. "I suppose he feels somewhat responsible, bringing the family to the island."

"Accidents happen," said Susan.

"He was very close with Parker, though, wasn't he?" asked Lucy, taking a wet glass off the rack and drying it.

"It's a terrible thing to lose a child," said Susan, rinsing off another tumbler. "A parent doesn't expect to outlive a child. It's not natural."

Lucy wanted to ask Susan if she thought that Scott had an unnatural, possibly incestuous relationship with Parker, but something in Susan's tone of voice indicated she had cut off that line of inquiry. Instead, she replaced the dry glass on its shelf and asked, in an offhand tone, if Parker had a special relationship with one of the men on the island. She knew the twins had mentioned seeing Parker with Will, but was hesitant to question Susan directly about her son.

"I wouldn't be surprised," said Susan. "Men are men and women are women and when there's not a lot to choose from, folks make do with what's available."

Lucy chuckled. "That sounds like the island motto: Make do with what's available."

"You said it," agreed Susan. "Like baked beans and brown bread. Tomorrow, if the chickens keep laying like they've been doing, maybe I can make a quiche." She

156

scrubbed at a stubborn bit of food stuck to a plate. "I'd kill a chicken, but then I'd just lose a layer."

"When you've got limited resources you've got to think about trade-offs and consider all the consequences," said Lucy, who was used to careful budgeting. Bill made a good living, but sometimes it was months between checks and she had to make sure the money lasted. "You've got to plan ahead. Winters here must be tough."

"Winter is the best time," said Susan, setting the last dish in the rack and moving on to the pans. "Plenty of peace and quiet, time to reflect and remember the ones who went before."

" 'The ones we love but see no more,' " said Lucy, quoting a phrase that was often used in the Sunday morning prayers at the Community Church.

"It's a funny thing," said Susan, wiping down the bleached wood counter, "but the ones I miss the most are the ones I fought with, the ones I didn't get along with. I guess I'm just quarrelsome and love a good fight."

"Well, thanks for the warning," said Lucy, folding the dish towel and hanging it on the wooden rack above the sink. "See you tomorrow."

"God willing," said Susan, stepping outside and closing the door behind her.

God willing, thought Lucy, wondering if it was simply a habitual phrase or if she meant something deeper. Was Susan simply fatalistic after living on the island for so long, or was she fearful that a killer was living among them? Nonsense, concluded Lucy, it was just a tossed off remark, like "God bless you" when someone sneezed, or her mother's favorite, "Onward and upward." Just something to say when you couldn't think of anything else.

It was too early to go to bed and Lucy didn't want to get involved with the scene in the living room, where exclamations of "No fair!" and "That's cheating!" from the conscious members of the family seemed to indicate they were carrying on as usual, playing some game or other, probably ignoring Scott, who was passed out on a sofa. She decided to step outside for a breath of fresh air.

Standing on the porch, she automatically glanced at the darkening sky, but no stars were visible, and neither was the moon. The fog, she realized, was thickening, shrouding the island in an even thicker and denser blanket of clouds. Nevertheless, she could see a blurry light at the old gardener's cottage. She felt a sudden need for company and decided to go and see if Ben or Wolf was available.

She could feel the chill dampness of the fog on her arms as she crossed the lawn, using the light as a beacon to guide her way. She paused midway to tighten a loose shoelace and began to wonder what she'd do if the light suddenly went out, and checked that the windows of the house were lit up. Who'd've thunk it, she marveled, that a simple electric porch light would seem so wonderful, even precious. A marvelous invention. You didn't realize how dark night could be until you spent a few on an island with limited electricity.

Reaching the gate in front of the gardener's house, she pushed it open and stepped into the glow of an old-fashioned kerosene lantern hanging from a hook on the porch. Wolf, who was stacking firewood, turned and greeted her with a toothy smile. Maybe she was simply reacting to his name, but she thought there was something wolfish in his expression. "What brings you out on this foggy night?" he asked, with only the slightest touch of a German accent.

"I'm just restless, I guess, and wanted a breath of fresh air."

"Very understandable," he said, carefully

placing a couple of split logs in a neat row on the stack. "I was told Scott's been drinking all day."

"He passed out at dinner."

"At the table?" asked Wolf, raising an eyebrow. He was awfully good looking if you overlooked those pointy werewolf teeth, thought Lucy, with his tanned face and sun-bleached hair and beard. He was fit, too, and tall with broad shoulders.

"No, he got up and stumbled into the living room, where he collapsed on a couch."

Wolf shrugged. "He's grieving. He really loved Parker."

"In a purely fatherly way?" asked Lucy.

Wolf seemed amused by the question, smiling as he considered the possibility. "That's a big thing now, there's a movement to expose every rich, old guy who's, what do you say, gone too far. . . ."

"Every day there's a new one, more shocking than the last," said Lucy.

"He is probably just like the rest, but I don't see him fooling with his daughters. He treated those girls, Parker especially, like little princesses. He was blind to their faults, thought they were angels and could do no wrong, especially Parker. That's why he's so upset."

"But what about the surviving members

of his family? It's not fair to the boys, or to Lily and Taylor. They need his love and support now more than ever."

"Maybe he'll come to realize that," said Wolf.

"If he sobers up," said Lucy. "I understand he's upset, but I suspect he's always been a heavy drinker."

Wolf gave her a wry smile and nodded.

"So how does he run his billion-dollar business if he's soused most of the time here on this island? It's really been bothering me."

"Well, he doesn't often spend so much time on the island; he usually just comes for weekends. He's got his own jet, flies into Islesboro on Friday afternoon. Will meets him there and they sail the Watson over."

"But the drinking?"

"He's got, what's the phrase, *folks*? He's got *folks*?"

"I think you mean *people*," said Lucy, smiling. "He's got people."

"Ja." Wolf leaned against the porch railing, crossing his arms. "Lots of people work for him, and it's safe to think they know what they're doing. By now he's mostly a figurehead, don't you think?"

"I guess." She seated herself on the porch steps, stretching out her legs. They were a bit tight and it occurred to her that she'd been doing a lot of walking. First thing in the morning she'd hiked out to the puffin nesting ground, then she'd hiked over to the farm, and she'd even played soccer with the boys. "I hadn't realized until now, but island life is pretty strenuous. You've got to walk everywhere, and things are far apart."

"Susan has a bicycle," said Wolf. "But there's only the one and she doesn't share."

"That's surprising," said Lucy, indulging in a bit of sarcasm. "She's such a soft touch."

Wolf laughed. "Funny. I hadn't noticed."

"So what's your impression? Is it really all one big, happy family here, billionaires and old-timers and hired workers, all getting along in this grand experiment of Scott's?"

"Pretty much, at least for me. Of course, I'm just here for the summer. I'm making good money, getting three meals a day, I don't have any complaints."

"But you'll be glad when September rolls around?"

"*Ja,* I miss my girlfriend."

"So you weren't tempted by the twins? From what I've heard, the boys told me that Parker and Taylor used to love sunbathing . . ."

"Some guys, maybe, but not me. I'm old-

162

fashioned. My girl is beautiful, but she doesn't flaunt herself. She's quiet, she sings in the church choir."

"What does she do when she's not singing?"

"University. She's studying chemistry."

"That's great," said Lucy. "Are you going to get married?"

"*Ja,* we're saving for a flat. We don't want a big wedding or a honeymoon. If you ask me, that's a big waste of money."

"And your girl is okay with this?" Lucy was skeptical.

"It was her idea."

"I wish you much happiness; she sounds like a treasure," said Lucy. "What about Will? I heard he had a thing going with Parker."

"I don't have too much contact with him; the Hopkinses are private." He shifted his weight from one foot to the other and stuffed his hands in the pockets of his jeans. "To tell the truth, I don't think they like me and Ben very much. They act like we don't know about boats because we're not native Mainers like them." He snorted. "I got news for them: Maine doesn't have a monopoly on boats. There's boats everywhere, and people who know how to sail them. And believe me, the first thing I learned about boating was how to make a boat fast to the dock because you really don't want it drifting off."

"So you think somebody untied the boats on purpose?" asked Lucy.

"I don't know what happened, but I do know that when I checked, and I check the dock every couple of hours, those boats were secure, they weren't going anywhere."

"Maybe the boys?" suggested Lucy. "Kids will be kids."

"Could be. If you ask me, I think they're pretty spoiled." Wolf picked up the lantern. "Do you want me to walk you back to the house?"

"Sure," said Lucy, grateful for the offer. "That would be great."

As they walked together, Lucy found herself shivering in the damp, chill air. "It makes you wonder," she mused aloud. "What's it like here in the winter? It must be awful, with the wind blowing off the Atlantic. How do the Hopkinses manage? Why do they do it?"

"They don't," said Wolf, laughing. "They've got a winter place in Florida."

CHAPTER TEN

Lucy thought about Wolf's parting comment as she prepared for bed. Her first reaction was surprise, shock even, and amusement, but the more she thought about it, the more troubled she became. What was real on the island, and what was fake? Here she'd thought Susan and Hopp and the boys were hardy, salt-of-the-earth Mainers who took pride in overcoming adversity. The sort of folks who loved to tell you about the winter when the snow reached the porch roof and all the pipes froze and they had to pull Ma's achy tooth out with pliers because they couldn't get to the dentist. And if she was all wrong about the Hopkinses, who apparently spent their winters in sunny Florida rather than battling the elements on the island, what else was she getting wrong?

Was everyone on the island putting on a big show? And who were they doing it for? She didn't really think it was for her benefit;

165

she was just a small-town reporter and it hardly mattered what she wrote in the *Pennysaver,* which was read by only a couple of thousand people at most. Was it for Scott? Or was it some sort of craziness that had seduced them all, like those tales of the Pied Piper or the emperor who had no clothes? Those stories ended with a shocking reveal, when the truth finally came out, and she wondered if the islanders were also in for something similar. Or was this make-believe so strong that nothing could shake it, not even Parker's death?

Finally tucked in bed, beneath the hand-made quilt, she looked around the room. Lily had told her it hadn't been changed since the house was built, in the late 1800s, and Lucy believed her. The beautiful blue and white wallpaper was clearly vintage, the substantial carved oak window and door casings, the crown molding and the twelve-inch baseboards spoke to an earlier time when craftsmanship was more highly prized. But it also seemed kind of weird, she thought, thinking of her own antique farm-house, which had undergone many changes through the years as modern advances like electricity, heating and indoor plumbing, TV and telephones were added. Windows were enlarged, closets were added to bedrooms, and fireplaces were boarded up. She and Bill had reversed some of the changes, like ripping up tatty carpeting to expose the original wood floorboards and uncovering the fireplaces, but others had been kept.

She liked some of the old ways. She'd enjoyed the quiet on the island, where motorcycles and souped-up cars never disturbed a peaceful evening. She liked the sense of coziness the oil lamps provided, and the crackle of a wood fire on a cool evening, but as the days passed she had an increasing sense of unreality and growing unease. It was all a bit too twee, too precious, and ultimately fake, she decided, as she slipped between the sheets and carefully blew out the bedside lamp.

Next thing she knew, it was morning. Not yet a bright morning, for sure, but definitely lighter than night. It must still be very early, she thought, intending to go back to sleep, but when she checked the bedside clock she was surprised to see it was almost eight. Hopping out of bed, she went to the window and saw the fog had increased; she couldn't even see the gazebo at the far edge of the lawn.

It was also quite chilly, she discovered, and hurried to dress in warm pants and socks, pulling on a sweater as she made her way to the bathroom. Downstairs in the dining room she found the twins quarreling over the last corn muffin. "Let's split it," she said, cutting the muffin in half and effectively ending the argument. "So what are you guys going to do today?" she asked, setting the plate down at her place and pouring herself a cup of coffee from a graniteware pot set on a Sterno burner. "Are you going out with Taylor to see the puffins?"

"Taylor promised," said Walter, taking a flaky biscuit from the bread basket and spreading jam on it.

"You know people used to eat puffins," said Fred. "I bet you'd eat one, Walter. You'd eat anything."

"I won't," countered Walter, taking a big bite and talking with his mouth full. "I like lots of foods, but I won't eat anything yucky."

"Name one thing you won't eat," challenged Fred.

"Poop! I won't eat poop, like you!"

"That's a lie!" exclaimed Fred, punching Walter in the arm.

"That's enough of that!" said Taylor, entering the room. "You're at the table, and we have a guest. Use your manners."

"Yeah," said Fred in a whiny voice. "Use

your manners or you can't go see the puffins."

"Uh, sorry boys. No can do," said Taylor,
joining them at the table. "It's too dangerous in this fog. I'm not even going myself.
The puffins will have to carry on without
us."

"Bummer," moaned Walter.

"Please, please, let us go," begged Fred.
"It's so boring here."

"Yeah, no fireworks, and now we can't
even go see the puffins."

"I know, guys. Be patient. The fog can't
last forever," said Taylor, lifting the cover off
a serving dish and helping herself to oatmeal. "I'll think of something you can do
instead."

"How about a scavenger hunt?" suggested
Lucy, who was helping herself to oatmeal
from a covered dish. "A July Fourth scavenger hunt. Maybe it will even become an
Independence Day tradition."

"Good idea," said Taylor, sprinkling brown
sugar on her oatmeal. "Lucy and I can make
a list of things for you to find."

"First one who completes the list is the
winner," said Lucy, reaching for the milk
pitcher. The endless supply of creamy goat's
milk was definitely one of the island's advantages.

"Is there a prize?" asked Fred.

"Oh, yes," said Lucy, remembering one summer she spent at her aunt's lake house when she got an entire tray of fudge for swimming all the way out to the dock and back. "You get fudge."

"How much fudge?" asked Walter.

"The whole batch," said Lucy.

"To share?" asked Fred.

"Only if you want to," said Lucy. "You could share, which would be the nice thing to do, or you could be selfish and hoard it all to yourself. It's up to you."

"I think the winner should definitely share," said Taylor.

The boys shared a look that seemed to indicate they didn't agree with their half sister.

"Let's say we start the hunt at ten," said Lucy, checking her watch. "That will give Taylor and me time to make the list."

"Okay!" chorused the twins.

"In the meantime, you boys can make your beds and tidy your room. I'll be up to check," said Taylor.

This time the okay was not quite as enthusiastic, but the two boys did shuffle off in the direction of their shared room. Taylor went to the sideboard and opened a drawer, producing a pad of paper and a pen, then returned to the table. Then the two women put their heads together to make a list of items they thought the boys could find on the island.

"It can't be too easy," said Lucy, "or they'll be done in five minutes."

"But we don't want it to be too hard so they get frustrated," said Taylor.

"And we don't want them venturing into dangerous areas, either," said Lucy.

The list grew quickly, including easy finds like a pinecone, a white pebble, and a green tomato, along with a few harder ones like a piece of sea glass, a crow's feather, and a tree fungus. They tried to construct the list so the boys would have to explore various areas on the island, including the farm, the dock, and the woods, all safe areas they were familiar with. Then Taylor went off to check that the boys had completed their morning chores, and when she returned and gave the all clear, Lucy rang the dinner bell announcing the beginning of the scavenger hunt.

Lucy and Taylor stood on the porch, watching as the boys conferred for a few minutes, then set off with lists and collection baskets in hand. "I guess I'd better get started on that fudge," said Lucy, suddenly painfully aware that she'd never made fudge in her life. "Do you think Susan has a recipe?"

"There's an old Fanny Farmer cookbook she swears by in the kitchen," said Taylor. "I'm sure it's got a recipe." She smiled, watching as Walter held up his first find, a big black crow's feather. "I'll keep an eye on the boys while you make the fudge."

There was no sign of Susan in the kitchen, but Lucy easily found the promised cookbook on a shelf next to the big black wood-stove. The recipe was simple enough, calling for cocoa powder, sugar, and butter, all items that were on hand. Corn syrup was optional, but advised, and she found a bottle of Caro in the pantry. The mixture was supposed to be cooked over a moderate heat until it reached the softball stage at 234 degrees, which could be determined by dropping a half teaspoon of candy into a cup of cold water or by using a candy thermometer. Lucy wasn't at all sure the cold-water method was reliable, but doubted such a thing as a candy thermometer was to be found in the kitchen. However, when she opened one of the big wooden drawers beneath the red linoleum counter-top, she found several.

Now, there was nothing further to do except to start, which she realized involved using the monster woodstove. Lucy realized she didn't have a clue. Did you add more wood and fire the thing up? Was it hot enough already? Cautiously holding her hand above the cook surface, she found it was only slightly warm, not what you'd call a moderate heat. She would certainly have to do something to make it hotter, but looking at the various doors with their polished chrome handles, she decided discretion was clearly the better part of valor. Even if she did manage to get the massive thing to work, she worried that she might cause some damage that would upset Susan. Or even worse, set off a chimney fire and burn down the house.

Heading back into the pantry, she poked around, hoping to find some alternative means of cooking, perhaps a fondue pot? She knew Susan used Sterno for the coffee warmer, maybe she could borrow that warmer and set a cook pot on it. She did find a couple of packages of Sterno, and was considering using one, when she noticed the familiar Coleman logo on a green enamel camp stove, neatly stored on a shelf, along with a couple of canisters of fuel.

Lucy seized her prize and set it up on the kitchen table, testing to make sure it worked. Sure enough, it gave a nice, even blue flame. Success! Soon she had a pot of fragrant chocolate syrup gently bubbling on the Coleman, and the mercury in the candy thermometer was steadily climbing to the desired temperature. When it reached the magic 234 degrees, Lucy removed the pot from the heat, dropped in two tablespoons of butter, and set it to rest until it was almost cold. Then she would add a teaspoon of vanilla, beat it until smooth and creamy, and pour it into a buttered pan to set.

She was so pleased with the result so far, that she considered the various options for improving the recipe, such as adding nuts or marshmallows. Nuts seemed risky, but marshmallows? She knew there were some in the pantry and she was pretty sure the winner would approve, and hopefully could be coaxed to share with his unsuccessful twin. Meanwhile, the fudge mixture was still quite hot, so she went out on the porch to check on the boys' progress.

At first there was no sign of them on the fog-shrouded lawn, but she waited patiently and eventually made out two dark, shadowy shapes. It was easy enough to identify them, as Walter was stockier and walked slowly with his head thrust out, looking down as he hunted, and Fred was thinner and tended to dash one way or another, until something caught his eye and he came to an abrupt stop. Lucy smiled, absorbed in watching them, until she suddenly remembered the unfinished fudge in the kitchen.

Finding the fudge had cooled, she added a handful of mini marshmallows and the vanilla and stirred enthusiastically until the mixture was no longer glossy and turned thick and creamy. She poured it onto a buttered pan to cool, as the recipe instructed, and scattered some red, white, and blue jimmies that she'd found on the shelf behind the marshmallows on top. She was just finishing up tidying the kitchen, replacing the Coleman stove in the pantry, when Susan arrived with a bowlful of fresh eggs.

"Nice batch of fudge," said Susan, with an approving nod.

"It's a prize for the boy who wins the scavenger hunt," said Lucy.

"Is that what they're up to?" asked Susan. "I noticed 'em running around like chickens with their heads cut off."

"Do chickens really do that?" asked Lucy, who had always wondered.

"I never saw one do it, I think it's just a saying," said Susan. "The boys are sure having a fine time, though. It's good for them to act like kids again."

"That's what I thought," said Lucy. "Do

you want some help with lunch?"

"Thanks," said Susan. "I'm just making egg salad sandwiches, there's some watermelon pickle in the pantry, and I guess I'll put out some of those cold beans from yesterday."

"Sounds good," said Lucy. "Maybe some hot tea?"

She watched as Susan expertly added wood and coaxed the old stove to life, setting the eggs to cook and kettle to boil. "I was terrified of that monster," said Lucy, confessing that she'd used the Coleman.

"Takes some getting used to," admitted Susan, who was spooning watermelon pickle into a pretty pressed glass dish. "I've got to admit, I kinda like the old thing. It gives off a nice heat on a cool day like this."

"But on a hot day?" asked Lucy. The devil whispered in her ear and she added, naughtily, "I suppose it's a bit like Florida in here then."

Susan didn't take the bait, but simply smiled and said, "You could say that."

Lucy didn't want to press the matter, so she asked if she should set the table.

"Please do. Luncheon plates are on the shelf here and let's see, we'll need places for six, four adults and the two boys, right?"

Lucy counted out six flow blue plates she

would have killed to own and carried them into the dining room, where she arranged them on the table. Silverware was in the sideboard and she put out salad forks next to the napkins, which were already set at each place, neatly refolded after breakfast and tucked into initialed silver napkin rings for the family members, and one engraved "guest" for her. They would be used again at dinner, too, but fresh napkins appeared each morning.

That job done, she returned to the kitchen, where Susan announced that lunch was ready and would she ring the bell, calling everyone to the table. Lucy stepped onto the porch and yanked the cord on the bell, expecting to see two hungry boys immediately materialize out of the fog that had settled onto the lawn. When that didn't happen, she rang the bell again, peering expectantly into the fog.

The screen door behind her opened, and Taylor stepped out. "Lunch is ready," she said.

"I know," replied Lucy. "Are the boys inside?"

"I haven't seen them," replied Taylor. "Haven't they come back?"

"No, I've rung the bell twice, but there's no sign of them. I thought you were going to keep an eye on them," said Lucy.

"Well, you know how kids are. Really fast. I stayed out for a while, but they went in different directions and, well, they know the island really well and I figured they didn't really need me. I wasn't doing much good anyway since I couldn't be in two places at once, so I came inside and put on some fresh nail polish." She held up her hands and wiggled her fingers, which were now tipped in bright orange paint. "Ocala Orange," she said. "I got sick of that tasteful ballet pink I've been using, I wanted something bold."

"It's certainly bold," agreed Lucy, thinking fleetingly that Florida seemed to be on a lot of people's minds. Then she returned to the problem of the missing boys. "What should we do?" she asked.

"Ring the bell again, and then let's go in and eat. They'll show up."

"What if they're in trouble?" asked Lucy.

"No way," said Taylor. "They're probably in the woods, or over by the farm and couldn't hear the bell. The fog muffles sound, you know. Trust me, they'll show up when they get hungry."

Lucy had her doubts, she'd never heard that fog muffled sound, but she figured Taylor knew more about conditions on the island than she did, and she certainly knew the boys' capabilities. "Okay," she agreed, sounding the bell once again.

And, once again, she scanned the mist-covered lawn, looking for two small, energetic boys to emerge from the fog.

"Come on inside," said Taylor, when the boys failed to appear. "There's no sense waiting out here. They're probably on their way, those boys never miss a meal."

Lucy let out a big sigh and followed Taylor into the dining room, where Scott and Lily were already sitting at their places. Scott, she noticed, was fingering an almost empty glass of whiskey, and Lily was slipping her napkin out of its ring. She looked up and smiled at Taylor and Lucy, and then noticed the boys' empty seats and furrowed her brow in concern.

"Where are the boys?" she asked.

CHAPTER ELEVEN

The question hung in the air for a few moments, as Lucy decided to let Taylor answer the question. She was only a guest, after all, and Taylor had been the one who was supposed to be keeping an eye on the boys. But Taylor remained silent.

"Did you ring the dinner bell?" demanded Lily.

"Several times, but they didn't come," said Lucy, feeling sick. What if something terrible had happened to the twins? The island was full of dangers: cliffs to fall from, ponds to drown in, and dangerous tides.

"It was Lucy's idea," said Taylor, reverting to playground rules. "She sent them out on a scavenger hunt."

"In this fog? Are you crazy?" demanded Lily, rising from her seat and glaring at Lucy.

Lucy felt she had to defend herself. "Taylor and I worked on it together," said Lucy.

"We were very careful when we made the list. We only included things that are easily available in safe locations. Pinecones and pebbles and stuff like that."

Lily was not impressed. "I can't believe you sent them outdoors in this dreadful fog. It was an insane thing to do. This island is dangerous."

"Lucy thought it would be fun for them and take their minds off Parker's death," said Taylor.

"Is this true?" asked Scott, rousing himself as the realization that his twin sons might be in trouble penetrated his alcoholic haze. "Are the boys out in the fog?"

"Taylor said they know every inch of the island and they'd be fine," said Lucy, who was beginning to feel she'd been conned and was now going to be the scapegoat. "And Taylor promised to keep an eye on them. Isn't that right?" she asked, turning to Taylor.

"What were you doing, Taylor?" demanded Scott. "Why didn't you watch the boys?"

"It was the fog," said Taylor. "I lost track of them."

"So why didn't you end the hunt right then?" asked Lily.

"Because they were having a good time,"

said Taylor. "I could hear them laughing and it's like Dad always says, the island is the boys' playground. I never thought they'd be in any danger."

Lily was incredulous. "Your sister just died falling off a cliff and you think this island is safe for two little eight-year-olds?"

"Don't point your finger at me!" snarled Taylor. "It's Dad who dragged us here. It's all his fault. Take it up with him. Meanwhile, instead of wasting time arguing, I'm going out to look for your kids — kids, by the way, that you've been ignoring for the last two days." She glared at Lily. "Parker was my sister, you know. She wasn't anything to you, she didn't even like you." With that, Taylor marched out of the dining room.

A glance at Lily made it clear that Taylor had scored a hit with her parting shot. She had turned pale and was hanging on to the back of a chair for support.

Lucy agreed with Taylor that nothing was to be gained by continuing to argue and started toward the door, intending to join her in searching.

"Hold on!" said Scott in a take-charge voice. "I'll get the men. We'll organize a systematic search." He paused, then added, "Lucy, see if you can catch Taylor. Tell her to come back. We'll start when everyone gets here and we have a plan."

Lucy obeyed, stepping outside onto the porch, where she found Taylor standing by the steps, looking out into the fog. "I don't know where to begin," she said, her voice breaking. "If only Parker was still alive . . ."

"Your father wants you to come back inside. He's going to get everyone together and organize the search."

"That's good," said Taylor. "I can't do it alone."

The two women had crossed the porch and almost reached the door when Scott barreled through, foghorn in hand. He let out three sharp blasts, paused, and repeated.

Miraculously, it seemed to Lucy, the islanders materialized out of the fog. First came Hopp, who had been working in the farm area, and Susan, who had been working upstairs in the house. Wolf came with an armload of firewood, and Brad appeared from inside the house carrying a pail of ashes from the fireplace. Ben arrived carrying a hoe on his shoulder, and Will was towing a cart containing garden produce, fresh milk, and eggs. They all gathered at the bottom of the porch stairs, awaiting instructions.

"We have an emergency situation," began Scott. "Fred and Walter didn't come home for lunch. . . ."

Hearing this, the islanders snapped to attention, ready to go into action.

"They went out this morning on a scavenger hunt and now we need to find them." He paused. "We should probably start by searching the perimeter of the island, in case they've fallen . . ."

"And the pond," suggested Susan, with a grim nod.

Oh, no, thought Lucy, feeling guilty about the pond. She should have warned the boys to stay away.

Scott nodded. "Right. So let's work in pairs: Susan, you go with Lucy and check the dock area and the pond; Ben and Wolf, take the west side, that's pretty rough; Taylor knows the north because of the puffins, Brad can go with her; Hopp and Will, take the barnyard and the south shore along to the old gardener's cottage. . . ."

Taylor interrupted her father. "Dad, I'd rather do the barnyard and the icehouse," she said. "I twisted my ankle yesterday and it's a little tender. I don't think it's a good idea for me to go all the way out to the puffins."

"Okay." Scott furrowed his brow, looking flummoxed. "So that means you and Brad have the farmyard, Hopp and Will can cover

184

the north side. I'll check the gazebo and then stay here at the house with Lily in case the boys show up. If you hear the foghorn, come back to the house, okay?"

It was then that Lily appeared on the porch, holding the plate of forgotten egg salad sandwiches. She was ghost-like, with pale skin and loose hair lifted by the slight breeze, her gauzy top fluttering around her. "Please take these, you'll need energy," she said, holding out the heavy platter with fragile, trembling arms.

A couple of the men grabbed sandwiches, but Lucy found she was no longer hungry. She was eager to begin searching.

"We best start with the dock," said Susan. "That's the likeliest place."

Lucy nodded and the two hurried across the lawn and made their way down the steep wooden stairs. Lucy bounded down, leaping from step to step, but Susan took the steps singly, leading with her left leg each time. "Bad knee," she explained, as Lucy waited for her at the bottom.

The dock was empty, but they walked to the end, scanning the water for any sign of the boys, fearing that one might have fallen in and the other gone in after him, thinking to save his brother.

"That's a relief," said Lucy, as they returned to the shore. "At least they didn't drown."

"Don't be too sure. It's deeper than you think there and they could be way under," said Susan, voicing her usual pessimism. "Takes a while for bodies to rise."

"Surely not," said Lucy. "They're good swimmers and it's not far to shore. Even if they did tumble in, they could pull themselves onto the dock."

Susan didn't seem convinced.

"I suppose if they hit their heads . . ." began Lucy.

"They'll never find them," said Susan, shaking her head.

"Don't say that!" Lucy was a big believer in positive thinking. "It's tempting fate."

"'Tisn't fate, it's little Charlie Rose."

"What? Who's that?"

"Little fella, same age as the twins. He was playing on the rocks, poking about in the tidal pools the way the kids do, on a beautiful summer day. His momma and poppa were watching, sitting on the cliff above, and never noticed it coming. 'Twas hard to see in the bright sunshine, with the light dancing on the waves. But it rolled in, a rogue wave, and it took little Charlie, carried him out to sea. Little tyke never had a chance."

"When was this?" asked Lucy, horrified.

"Oh, some time ago. Back in the nineteen thirties I think."

"And they never found him?"

"No, but he lives on, a ghost in the water. He's always waiting, ready to seize unwary wanderers. He wants company, playmates, down there, in the deep."

"That's just a story," said Lucy. "There are no ghosts in the deep."

"Think what you want," said Susan, dismissively, "but they never found little Charlie, and I'll wager they never find Fred and Walter, either."

Lucy was growing tired of Susan's nonsense and said so. "You surely don't believe a silly old story like that," she said, whirling around on the pebble and shell–strewn beach and confronting Susan. "It's ridiculous."

"Don't be so sure, missy," replied Susan. "There's things we ken not. . . ."

"Oh, cut it out," snapped Lucy, who had had more than enough of Susan's gloom and doom. "You don't fool me with all this old-timey stuff. You're a thoroughly modern woman; you don't even stay here year-round, do you? You go off to Florida every winter, that's what I hear."

Susan looked down at her feet, clad in a

pair of faded red Keds. "You're right," she said, with a wry twist of her lips. "I only talk like my grandma because Scott likes it. And Hopp and I do go to Florida for the winter, you're right about that, too. He's getting on in years, and can't take the cold, and I don't like being all alone out here, what with the boys being gone so much. It was different when there were other people on the island; then we were part of a nice, little community. There were potlucks and card games, and there was always somebody to help out when you needed something." She shrugged. "I do miss the change of seasons, I do. I can't say I really like Florida, but like Hopp says, it's better than the alternative. And there are a lot of Mainers, snowbirds like us, down there, so it's not so bad except for Christmas." She shook her head. "It doesn't seem like Christmas at all when you're wearing shorts and sweating to beat the band."

"I suppose not," said Lucy, as they followed a well-worn path that led from the little beach upward through a scrubby, rocky bank toward the pond.

When they finally reached the pond, it was shrouded in fog like the rest of the island and scraps of mist hung over the gray water. It was mostly surrounded by pinewoods, but boulders strewn along the shore provided access for those who were nimble enough to leap from stone to stone. Lucy suspected the twins would have no trouble at all as they hunted for frogs and turtles, or fished for minnows.

Susan remained on the path that ran alongside part of the pond, but Lucy stepped onto a flat rock and peered into the water, surprised to see several large goldfish appear by her feet. They remained there, waggling their tails, as if expecting to be fed.

"There's goldfish!" she exclaimed.

"Yeah, somebody put 'em in there years ago," said Susan. "Don't know why."

"Maybe had them for pets and let them go at the end of the summer," guessed Lucy. "Or maybe it was a prank."

"They do fine in there, but the boys do like to feed them, they give them stale bread," said Susan, looking around. "Was there anything on that list that would've brought the boys here?"

"I don't think so," said Lucy. "No goldfish, nothing alive, for that matter. We didn't want them trapping live creatures. It would've been cruel."

"It gets pretty deep in the middle," said Susan, gazing out over the glassy surface of

189

the water.

"Any lovestricken maidens down there, who drowned themselves?" asked Lucy, unable to resist teasing Susan.

"Not so far as I know," said Susan, sounding a bit miffed. "People did used to skate here in winters past. But I never heard of anybody falling through the ice."

"Did they cut the ice?" asked Lucy, remembering an exhibit in the Tinker's Cove Historical Society picturing old-timers cutting out blocks of ice that they would store in icehouses for use in the summer.

"Oh, yes. That's why the pond is here. They dug it out, made it bigger, so they could harvest the ice."

"What about now?" asked Lucy, thinking of the icehouse containing Parker's body.

"Scott has ice brought over from the mainland; Hoyt's sells big blocks that they put in the icehouse."

Lucy nodded and jumped off her rock, joining Susan on the path. The two walked on, following the cart track that led back to the farmyard, studying the ground for any sign of the boys. Lucy found herself saying a little prayer, over and over. *Just one sign, please. A dropped candy wrapper, a scrap of comic book, anything. Please.* But there was nothing that indicated the boys had been there.

Susan suddenly stopped, put her hands on her hips, and yelled, "Fred! Walter! Come on out. Fred! Walter!" Receiving no answering yell, she sighed and lowered her head.

"I feel awful about this," said Lucy. "I never thought there was any danger. I thought they'd run around for an hour or so and come back with their collections, eager to show what they'd found and claim the prize." She paused. "I thought they might fight over the fudge, that worried me, and I was hoping I could convince the winner to share. I don't know why I didn't make two pans, it's not like they'd know how big a batch of fudge really is. I guess I would've decided to cut it up, anyway, and that would've solved the problem." She was rambling, thinking aloud. "The fudge was not the problem, it was the fog. Sending the boys out into the fog. Lily was right, I must have been crazy or something."

"You shouldn't blame yourself," said Susan. "Scott encouraged the boys to run free. He read some book about helicopter parenting and concluded kids should be free range, like chickens. Free to explore and test themselves." She snorted as an ear-shattering scream pierced the quiet and a red-tailed hawk flapped into view in the sky right above them. "Problem with free range is you can lose a few chickens to the hawks."

"Boys are smarter than chickens, though. Right?"

"Hopefully," said Susan.

"And hawks don't attack boys," said Lucy, who was beginning to think that perhaps there was a predator on the island who was more dangerous than a redtail. The thought had occurred to her earlier, that Scott might have an enemy who was lying undercover on the island, waiting to inflict damage on his target by kidnapping his sons. Now that she knew the island was bigger than she thought, and mostly covered with thick woods, his fears about possible intruders seemed a bit more realistic.

Lucy had a deep conviction, nourished by her Sunday school teachers, that the love of money was the root of all evil. Didn't the Bible say that it was harder for a rich man to enter heaven than for a camel to go through the eye of a needle? The eye of a needle, she knew from reading *National Geographic* magazine as a child, was actually a small opening in an ancient wall, but definitely too small for a camel. She had long harbored a distrust of extremely wealthy people, figuring they must have broken a few rules and cheated a few people in order to amass their incredible fortunes.

So even though she was impressed by Scott Newman's commitment to saving the environment, she doubted that he had always played by the rules as he emerged from business school laden with college debt and began his ascent into the Fortune 500. He had admitted that he most likely had made some enemies along the way, and his environmental stance had probably earned him a few more. Maybe she'd read too many thrillers and seen too many movies, but it didn't seem entirely impossible that some rival might have hired a hitman to even the score against Scott.

Her thoughts were running along those lines, thinking of oil cartels and chemical corporations, when the foghorn suddenly sounded.

"Praise God," shouted Susan. "They've been found."

"Thank heaven," said Lucy. "I hope they're all right."

The two women hurried, running with renewed energy along the path, joining up with Ben and Wolf when they reached the meadow and hurrying on past the enormous flower garden. The four burst out onto the lawn and headed straight for the porch stairs, where they joined the others gathered there: Hopp and Will, Brad and Taylor.

Looking around, Lucy was dismayed to see no sign of the boys. No matter, she thought, imagining they were probably inside, being fussed over by Lily and treated to cookies and milk.

The door opened and Scott stepped out, but instead of the expected smile he looked grim. Stepping to the edge of the porch, he held up a worn kid's sneaker with a Velcro strap. "Hopp found this on the path by the greenhouse," he said. "But that's all. The boys are still missing."

CHAPTER TWELVE

Seeing the downcast and discouraged expressions on the searchers' faces, Scott was quick to offer encouragement. "This is not the news we were all hoping for, but it is a good sign and gives us an indication of the boys' location. I suggest we take a short break, I know most of us haven't eaten for some time, and after refueling we'll focus our search on the southern side of the island, especially the rocky area between the gardener's cottage and the gazebo. Agreed?"

There were nods and murmurs of assent from the small group gathered on the lawn.

"Susan, do you think you could put something together for these folks?" asked Scott, as members of the group began to seat themselves on the lawn. Some, like Ben, even flopped down and sprawled on the grass.

"Sure thing," said Susan, who was quickly joined by Lucy. The two were walking around the porch, to the kitchen door, when Lily suddenly exploded from the front door and practically knocked them down. Lucy stepped aside as the distraught woman ran on, her hair flying and those gauzy sleeves fluttering, looking like an avenging angel about to unleash thunderbolts and lightning strikes of righteous anger.

"This is all your fault!" she screamed, confronting Scott. "You're the one who put the boys in danger, you with all your talk of building independence and encouraging risk taking!"

She raised her fists, intending to strike her husband, but Scott grabbed her by the wrists. "I know you're upset . . ." he began.

Twisting free, Lily glared at him. "Upset doesn't begin to describe it! You're completely irresponsible. You're always spouting off, but you don't take responsibility. Believe me, if something has happened to those boys, I'm through." She shook her head. "Maybe it's already over and I was too dumb to see it."

Scott looked as if he'd been slapped. "Lily, this isn't the time . . ."

"It's definitely time," snapped Lily, turning on her heels and marching inside, leaving her husband alone on the porch.

"She's upset," he said, speaking to the

crew. "She doesn't mean it." Then he pulled a map of the island out of his pocket and plopped down on one of the wicker chairs, studying it.

Lucy followed Susan into the kitchen, where they began assembling peanut butter and jelly sandwiches.

Lucy's mind was miles away as she made a big pot of tea and filled a basket with chocolate bars, stocked in the pantry along with graham crackers and marshmallows for s'mores, which Lucy intended for the searchers to carry along with them.

"It's pretty rugged down there, they might need some extra energy," said Susan, approvingly.

Lucy nodded, remembering the dread she felt when Zoe, only three years old, disappeared while she was shopping in a big box store. One minute the little girl was beside her as she searched through a bin of cheap flip-flops for her size, and then she wasn't. Suddenly panicked, Lucy searched the nearby area, thinking the child couldn't have gone far in the few minutes she was distracted.

Finding no trace of her daughter among the racks of cheap shoes, she headed for the toy department, thinking the little one might have gone there. But again, there was no sign of Zoe by the displays of dolls and stuffed animals.

Now, truly desperate with anxiety, Lucy feared Zoe had been lured away by a stranger, some sick pedophile who preyed on innocent children. She was racing through the aisles, calling Zoe's name, when a store manager confronted her. "Can I help you?"

Lucy grabbed the manager by the arms. "My daughter's missing. She's only three."

"We'll find her," said the manager, using her walkie-talkie to order several associates to place themselves by the doors and to question anyone leaving with a young child. "Can you describe her?" she asked.

"Three years old, dark brown hair," said Lucy.

"Her clothing?"

Lucy struggled to remember what Zoe was wearing, then suddenly remembered arguing that morning over Lucy's suggested outfit. "A shirt with a glittery unicorn, she insisted," said Lucy, blinking back tears and wishing she hadn't made such a fuss about it. "She wouldn't wear anything else."

The manager's voice on an intercom suddenly filled the store, asking anyone who saw a dark-haired three-year-old girl wearing a unicorn shirt to immediately inform the nearest sales associate. Then they waited.

It seemed an eternity, but Lucy knew it was only a matter of minutes before the manager's walkie-talkie buzzed and a scratchy voice said the little girl had been found in the pet department. Lucy followed the manager through the maze of aisles filled with everything from jumbo bottles of dish soap to fishing rods and, there in a huge dog bed, they found Zoe, fast asleep.

"You know," she said to Susan, as she filled a huge teapot with boiling water, "I bet those boys got tired and curled up somewhere."

"Could be," agreed Susan, slapping the last sandwich on a platter. "While the others are focused on the shore, I think we should search in the old village."

"Old village?" asked Lucy, hoisting a heavy tray containing the teapot, cream, and sugar, as well as mugs and the basket of candy bars, and following Susan, who was carrying the big platter of sandwiches.

"Yeah," she replied, opening the screen door and holding it for Lucy. "It's on the west end of the island; nobody lives there anymore. There are lots of hidey-holes there."

"That sounds like a real possibility," said

Lucy, as they set the food down on a white wicker porch table.

She waited as the others served themselves, then poured herself a mug of tea and grabbed a sandwich. She barely tasted it as she bolted it down, and when she gulped the tea it burned her mouth, but she didn't notice. She was thinking of the amazing sense of relief she'd felt when she saw her little girl in that green plaid doggy bed.

It didn't take long for the sandwiches and candy to disappear and the teapot to empty, and the searchers were ready to resume their mission. As before, Scott referred to the map and pointed out various areas for each pair of rescuers to search. Lucy and Susan were initially assigned to take another look at the farmyard, which had already been searched by Brad and Taylor, but when Susan suggested the old village, he gave his assent.

"I hadn't thought of that, but the boys were fascinated with that place," he said, also sending Taylor and Brad along with them.

Susan led the way, taking them only a short distance along the well-trod path that was the island's main thoroughfare and veering off northward past the ice pond, following an overgrown path that seemed to be little more than a deer track. As she struggled along, pushing away weeds and vines, Lucy wondered if there were deer on the island, and if so, how they got there.

"There's deer, and rabbits, mice and voles," answered Susan.

"Even coyotes," said Taylor.

"But it's an island," protested Lucy. "How did they get here?"

"They hop from island to island, they don't necessarily come all the way from the mainland in one go," explained Taylor. "And a few hitchhike, unwittingly find themselves on a boat, or a piece of driftwood."

"Don't forget the ice," said Susan. "Doesn't happen now, least not that I can recall, but in winters past, they say the ice pack sometimes came all the way out to the island."

"That's a lot of ice," said Lucy, who remembered seeing the entire harbor in Tinker's Cove frozen solid during one particularly bitter winter.

It didn't take long to reach the old village, which Lucy wouldn't have recognized as a human habitation unless she'd been told. No houses remained standing, as the departing residents had stripped their homes of windows, doors, and anything else that could conceivably be carried away. The

201

remaining islanders had used the wood shingles and framing for firewood, leaving little except the brick-lined cellar holes and chimneys.

"Be careful," warned Susan, "there's old wells and cesspits about that you don't want to fall into. Better find a good, sturdy stick to test the ground and make sure it's solid."

Lucy was horrified. "Could that have happened to the boys? Could they have fallen into an old well?"

Susan shrugged and stripped leaves and small branches from a fallen bough. "Hope not, but it's a possibility."

Brad and Taylor ignored Susan's advice and immediately began exploring the perimeter of the village. Lucy followed her example and looked for a similar stick, which she soon found. Then she and Susan advanced together, in the opposite direction, circling the village. When the two pairs completed searching the exterior, they moved into the interior, checking each cellar hole as they went, as well as the occasional tumbledown shed that had been overlooked by the scavengers.

Seeing Brad and Taylor duck into one of the sheds, Lucy feared the rickety structure might collapse on top of them and hurried after them, intending to warn them of the danger. When she approached, however, she heard raised voices, as if they were arguing. She listened, trying to make out what they were fighting about, but could only make out a few curse words and insults.

She was about to announce her presence with a cough, when Taylor suddenly ducked out of the tiny, overgrown building. Startled to see Lucy, she quickly said, "Outhouse," brushing cobwebs off her hair.

"The seats are still there if you want to use it," added Brad, with a smirk, emerging after her.

"I'll pass," said Lucy. "Any sign of the boys?"

The two shook their heads and moved on, continuing their search and calling the boys' names. Then they'd stop and listen, hoping even for a faint "help," but there was no sound but the occasional rustling of leaves, lifted by the slightest of breezes.

Lucy was exhausted when Susan finally announced that they'd searched every bit of the old village and it was time to head back to the house so she could start cooking supper. "You can stay if you want and keep looking," she told the others, "but I don't think there's any point." She shook her head. "They're not here."

Lucy had the odd sensation of being

covered with sweat from the exertion of climbing in and out of cellar holes, scrambling over rocks, and dragging vines and branches out of the way, but also chilled from the damp fog. The humidity, she figured, was near one hundred percent due to the fog, but the temperature remained low and was probably barely seventy. The air was still and heavy, and her legs felt heavy, as if she were walking underwater all the way back to the house.

"You look done in," said Susan, when Lucy hauled herself up the five or six steps to the porch. "You should lie down for a bit and rest."

"Nonsense. I'll help you with supper."

"No need," insisted Susan. "It's under control."

"Are you sure?" asked Lucy, who was torn. She wanted nothing more than to lie down on her bed, every bone and muscle in her body was screaming for rest, but she suspected Susan was every bit as exhausted as she was.

"Yup, I'm gonna make my five-ingredient chili and throw together a batch of corn bread, nothing to it." She nodded, and Lucy thought she looked as if she'd aged about ten years since the morning. "Come down in half an hour and set the table for me, that would be a big help, and you can do the dishes, too."

"You've got a deal," said Lucy, feeling better about her nap.

She climbed the stairs slowly, leaning on the carved wood railing for support, and went straight to her room. There she set the alarm on her windup clock for half an hour, then flopped back onto her pillow. Too tired to move, even to cover herself with the afghan on the foot of the bed, she was out like a light until the alarm went off.

She bolted upright and reached for the clock, trying to recall what she was doing in bed at a quarter to six. Then the whole horrible, dreadful reality hit her, and she wished she could close her eyes and go back to sleep and forget everything. But she couldn't do that. Walter and Fred were missing and she had to do what she could to help, even if it was only setting the table and washing the dishes. So she got up and stretched, paid a visit to the bathroom, and went downstairs. As she descended she felt a faint flutter of hope: Maybe there had been a new development while she slept, maybe the boys had been found.

Stepping into the kitchen, she quickly abandoned that idea. Susan was sitting at the table, her face in her hands, a crumpled

205

handkerchief lying on the table in front of her. Then it struck Lucy that perhaps the boys had been found injured or even dead.

Her voice was little more than a croak when she asked, "Any news?"

Susan looked up and shook her head.

Lucy was immediately relieved; then her spirits sank as she realized nothing had changed. "Well, you go on home," she said. "I can take it from here."

Susan pushed against the table with her hands and got up slowly, painfully. "The corn bread is in the oven, it'll be done in five minutes or so, and the chili's in that stewpot on the stove. Put out a pitcher of water, though they'll probably want something stronger." She allowed herself a disapproving sniff. "They probably won't have much appetite, but at least they'll have something to pick at."

"I'm really hungry," said Lucy.

Susan looked at her. "Yeah, well, you've been scrambling over this island all day looking for the boys, unlike some who just sat home, emptying the whiskey bottle."

Interesting reaction, thought Lucy, thinking that there was definitely a sense of resentment buried under Susan's seemingly endless willingness to please the Newmans. Not that she thought Susan or any one of the Hopkinses would hurt the boys. But Scott, he was a different story, and she wouldn't be surprised if one day Susan snapped and exacted revenge. Probably something petty, like pushing pins into a voodoo doll, that would give her a sense of power over her boss.

"Go on, shoo," said Lucy, taking an apron off the hook and waving it at Susan.

"Okay," said Susan. "See you in the morning." She sighed. "Hopefully, things will be brighter then."

Lucy smiled and nodded as she reached for the dinner plates, counting out six and then realizing, with a sob, that she needed only four. It took no time at all to set the table, which looked too large without the boys' places. Then she pulled the pan of corn bread out of the oven, letting it cool while she transferred the chili to the tureen Susan had left on the counter. She cut up the warm corn bread and piled it in the napkin-lined basket that was set out ready for it, then carried the food to the table. She hesitated about ringing the dinner bell, which somehow seemed unseemly, and as it happened she didn't have to. Taylor appeared and offered to let her parents know the meal was ready.

Soon they were gathered at the table, and

Lily suggested saying grace.

"Do you really think that will help?" demanded Scott.

"It can't hurt," snapped Lily, bowing her head.

Scott refused, but Lucy and Taylor also bowed their heads as Lily began to offer thanks for the meal. "And, Lord, please remember my little boys, Fred and Walter, and keep them safe through the night."

"Amen," said Lucy, blinking back tears.

"Enough!" snarled Scott. "Pass the corn bread."

They busied themselves filling their plates with food, then ate in silence until Taylor spoke up. "Do you think the boys could be playing a trick on us?" she asked.

"Well, if they are, it's certainly gotten out of hand," said Scott, slathering butter on his corn bread.

"I'm afraid they've had a terrible accident," said Lily, who was crumbling her corn bread with trembling hands. "That's the only explanation I can think of."

"Really? You don't think *they* might have kidnapped them, to get back at me. I have a lot of enemies, you know. *They'd* like to get me."

"Who are your enemies?" asked Lucy. "Business competitors?"

Scott furrowed his brow and leaned forward, resting his elbows on the table. "They're all out to get me. Because I'm successful and I'm challenging the power structure. They don't care about the environment, about pollution. Do you know there's a floating island of trash in the Pacific Ocean that's as big as Texas? That's what they want to keep doing, making plastic and pumping oil and fracking natural gas, filling the air with poison and dumping trash into the sea. And it's not just the environment, it's our minds, too. They control the air waves and send out evil messages that clutter up our brains and make us fearful. I'm the only one who sees it, who calls *them* out, and that's why *they* want to get me."

"Scott, you know you're full of bull," said Lily. "Nobody's out to get you."

He glared at his wife. "You're so naïve. Don't you see? Somebody here broke the rules and went on the grid, that's how *they* found us. It wouldn't be hard to snatch those boys. Guys in wetsuits, ex-Navy Seals, in a Zodiac, in a matter of minutes they could have grabbed the boys and been gone."

Lucy could picture such a scenario, she'd seen it in lots of movies and TV shows. But that was fiction, right?

"If you say so," said Lily, sighing and abandoning her plate of crumbled corn bread. "I'm not hungry." She stood up. "Lay off the scotch, okay?" Then she left the dining room on footsteps so light it hardly seemed as if she'd been there at all.

"Lily's got a point, Dad," said Taylor, speaking to her father. "The scotch doesn't help."

"It helps me," said Scott, draining his glass and getting up, heading to the bar in the living room.

"Well, looks like it's just you and me," said Taylor, giving Lucy a grim little smile, and helping herself to a second serving of chili.

"Do you have any ideas about what happened to the boys?" asked Lucy. "Do you think your father is right and they might have been kidnapped?"

"Beats me," said Taylor. "Anything's possible, I suppose."

Lucy turned her attention to her dinner, and her thoughts to Scott's crazy rant. That's what it was, she decided, nothing more. There was no evil cabal out to destroy him, or the environment. The way she saw it, people tended rather selfishly to pursue their own interests. She cared about the environment, but sometimes she bought plastic bottles of water or paper plates because it made sense in her life. If there was an affordable and ecological alternative, she'd probably choose it, but most often there wasn't. And as for the CEOs and stockholders of big companies, well, they wanted to make a profit, and they would most likely continue to do damage to the environment until it became unprofitable to do so.

Taylor broke into her thoughts. "Well, thanks for dinner," she said, rising from her chair and leaving the table.

Lucy wondered why the girl assumed she was responsible for the meal, or why she didn't feel any need to offer to help clean up. Somehow she no longer considered Lucy an honored guest, but a servant. So that's what being helpful gets you, she thought, beginning to clear the table. But as she carried the dirty dishes into the kitchen, Lucy's thoughts returned to Scott's crazy theory. One thing struck her as not so crazy, and that was his idea that somebody had gone online. That seemed to indicate that he suspected there was a phone or computer or some sort of device on the island. But if there was, why wasn't it being used to call for help?

CHAPTER THIRTEEN

Lucy busied herself with the dishes, concentrating on the job at hand and letting go of the unwanted and unsettling thoughts and images that flitted through her mind. While she scrubbed out the pans and brushed the tablecloth and wiped the counter, her subconscious went to work and she suddenly had a plan, which she decided to carry out immediately.

When she entered the living room she was pleased to see her quarry was already there, sitting on a sofa, and was alone. "Take a seat," said Taylor, looking up from the tattered old *Town & Country* magazine she was reading.

"I'm tired, but I know I won't be able to sleep tonight," said Lucy, seating herself on the opposite sofa. "How about you?"

"Same," said Taylor. "I usually play a relaxing guided meditation on my phone, but I can't do that here."

Lucy looked around, making sure they were still alone. "That's what I've been meaning to ask you," said Lucy, whispering. "You've got a cell phone, right?"

Taylor was quick to deny it. "No way," she said. "Dad would kill me."

Lucy didn't believe her denial for a minute. "I've got two daughters about your age and I swear, those phones are glued to their hands. And," she added, "it's easy enough to conceal one."

"Okay," admitted Taylor, in a whisper. "I do have a phone. I knew Dad would take mine, he always collects them all in a big, stupid ceremony, but I bought another that I kept." She shook her head. "Not that it's done me much good. I can't get a signal out here."

"You've been trying to get help?"

"Oh, yeah. This is nuts, storing poor Parker's body in the icehouse. Everybody's forgotten about her, because of the boys, but she's still gone and we ought to be planning her funeral. And now the boys have disappeared and we're tramping all over the island, probably destroying any evidence that might help find them. The police know how to search properly, and we need help. Things are out of control, this is not normal, but somehow we've all drunk the Kool-Aid and are playing along with Dad's craziness. We're all hostage to his paranoid delusions."

"Maybe we should confront your father, all together. A united front."

Taylor shook her head. "Lily tried at supper. You saw how that went over, she doesn't have any influence over him." She paused. "He can get violent, you know, if he's pushed too far. We've all been bruised at one time or other, and he broke Lily's jaw once."

"I had no idea," said Lucy, shocked to her core.

"We're all afraid of him," said Taylor, seeming to shrink into her seat as heavy footsteps were heard in the hallway. She looked straight into Lucy's eyes and pleaded, "You won't tell him about my phone, will you?"

"Of course not," said Lucy. "You can count on me."

"Thanks," whispered Taylor, as Scott pushed the door open and entered the room.

"Thanks for what?" he demanded.

"Thanks for passing the magazine," said Taylor, smoothly. "That's all, Dad. I just wanted something to read."

"Oh." He looked around the room, then sat down heavily in a big armchair. "Taylor, get that hassock for me, okay?"

Taylor was on her feet in an instant. "Sure thing, Dad," she said, shoving the hassock toward him and lifting his legs one at a time, easing his feet onto it.

"That's better," he said, relaxing into the chair and folding his hands on his stomach. Moments later, he was snoring loudly.

"I guess I'll go to my room, where it's quiet," said Taylor, giving her father a disapproving look.

"I'll go up, too," said Lucy, getting up and climbing the stairs with Taylor. When they reached the landing, Taylor went into the bathroom and Lucy went into her room. Once inside, she decided it was still early enough for the second part of her plan, and grabbed her flashlight and a warm sweater against the evening chill. Then she left her room, noticing that Taylor was apparently running a bath as she passed the bathroom and went downstairs. She was in the hallway and headed for the door when Lily appeared, a wraithlike figure in a filmy white negligee, clutching a fat photo album to her chest.

"Lucy, won't you look at these pictures with me?" she pleaded, placing her hand on Lucy's arm. "We had such happy times."

This wasn't Lucy's plan for the evening,

but she couldn't bring herself to refuse. "Of course," she said, slipping the mini flashlight into her hip pocket.

Lily led the way past the living room, where Scott could be heard snoring heavily, to the dining room, where she chose a chair and sat down, setting the album on the table. She patted the chair next to hers, indicating Lucy should sit there, and when Lucy was seated she opened the album.

"That's me, in the hospital, with the boys," she said, smiling and pointing to a photo of her smiling self holding a swaddled and hatted newborn in each arm. "Scott took the picture, that's why he's not in it."

"They look quite big for twins," said Lucy.

"Oh, they were. About six pounds each. I was huge, you can't imagine how big my belly was." Lily turned the page. "And here they are, snuggled together in a bassinet. That's what I did, at first, kept them together."

"Now they seem quite different," said Lucy. "Walter's a bit reserved and Fred's got a lot of enthusiasm."

"You're so right," said Lily, "you must be a keen observer." She was flipping through the pages, looking for a certain photo. "Here we are," she said, pointing to a photo of the two boys, each in a separate high chair, with a birthday cake set on the tray. "Their one-year birthday," she said. "We didn't even have time to snap the photo before Fred had grabbed a fistful of cake, but Walter, he only dabbed a bit of icing on his finger and licked it."

It was true. Fred's face and most of the rest of him was covered with smashed birthday cake, while Walter was focused on examining the icing decorations on his cake. Lucy was still looking at the photo, trying to think of something to say, when Lily suddenly slammed the album shut. "I've been kidding myself, thinking Scott brought us to the island because he really believes this old-fashioned lifestyle is good for the family." She shook her head. "It's not about family at all, it's about his paranoid ideas. And now look where he's got us. Parker's dead, the boys are missing, and we have no way to get help. And even if we could call for help, I'm not sure he'd allow it." Her voice dropped. "I think he needs psychiatric help."

"I think you're right," said Lucy.

"Should I have him committed? Is such a thing possible?"

"Probably. You'd need a lawyer."

"Scott has lawyers; they'd oppose it, I'm sure."

"Most likely," admitted Lucy. "But it's worth trying if you think he's a danger to himself or others. That's the standard."

Lily pressed her lips together and wrung her hands. "He's dangerous, all right. Sometimes I really think he might have killed the boys." She raised her head and brushed her tears away. "It happens, sometimes. Parents do kill their children, they do. Not because they're cruel, but because they're deluded and they think the children will be better off out of this evil world; they want them to be safe in heaven." A silver-framed photo of Scott caught her eye. "Sometimes it's because they want to hurt the other parent, or they think of the children as rivals who are getting all the love."

Too much information, thought Lucy, who usually loved interviewing people and learning something she'd never suspected, like the minister who played sexy blues in a nightclub on Saturday nights, or the travel agent who confessed she was terrified of flying. Tonight, she was truly sorry she'd been given this glimpse of Lily's darkest fears.

"I honestly don't think he would do anything like that," she said, patting Lily's hand. "We have to have faith that this will work out, that the boys will be found. We have to keep looking, and remember, the ferry is coming in two days. Help is on the way, we just have to carry on until then."

"I pray you're right," said Lily, clasping Lucy's hands and hanging on for dear life. "You know my worst fear? That he'll lock us all up and put on a big show that everything's all right. And the ferry will drop off the supplies and sail away and we'll be stuck here with the King of the Quahog Republic."

"That's not going to happen," said Lucy, with steely determination. "I'll make sure it doesn't."

"How can you do that?" asked Lily, sounding doubtful. "Scott has guns and isn't afraid to use them. He won't want police and investigators on the island, raking up his past and poking into his business. Do you have a plan?"

"Not yet," admitted Lucy, somewhat daunted, "but I'm working on it."

"Bless you," said Lily, gazing intently into Lucy's eyes and grasping her hands.

Lucy withdrew her hands awkwardly and stood up, pushing her dining chair behind her, which caused it to fall backward with a bang. Panicked, Lily jumped to her feet. "Damn, now you've woken him."

They both listened intently, reassured when the snores continued, uninterrupted, from the next room.

Lily let out a big sigh of relief, while Lucy righted the chair. "That was a close one," she said, placing her hand over her heart.

"Everything will be all right," said Lucy, who wasn't at all sure it would be, but wanted to comfort Lily. As for herself, she wanted to get out of the house as fast as she could. It was all getting very weird and she needed to get some distance, some fresh perspective. "I'm going out for a bit," she told Lily. "I need some fresh air."

"Out?" Lily's pale eyebrows shot up. "You're going outside?"

"Not far, I won't go far," promised Lucy. It was an easy promise, after all, considering she was on a fairly small island.

"Do you really think you should?" Lily had lowered her voice and was leaning forward.

"I'll be fine," insisted Lucy. "It's still light."

"It's dangerous out there. Just think what happened to Parker" — her voice broke — "and the boys."

"I'll be careful," promised Lucy, breaking away and walking briskly toward the door. For a moment she feared it might be locked, that she might be trapped inside, but when she reached for the heavy brass knob it turned and the huge door swung open. *Get a grip,* she told herself, determined to resist the paranoia that seemed to be infecting the house. *This isn't an Agatha Christie story; people aren't going to disappear one by one, slain by a killer intent on avenging a past wrong.*

But what if she was mistaken, she thought, as she crossed the lawn, heading for the gazebo where . . . what? Where she hoped to hail a passing boat? Or to enjoy the non-existent, fog-shrouded view? What exactly was she going to do? Because it now seemed to her that every day that brought the ferry's arrival closer was a day that put her in even more danger. Not only her, but everyone on the island who was a threat to whoever was behind Parker's death and the boys' disappearance. She had to send out a call for help immediately; she couldn't afford to wait for the ferry.

Her only hope, she decided, was if the Hopkinses had a marine radio hidden away somewhere on the island, and if she could convince them to use it. It was a risky move, if they were the ones behind it all, but that was a risk she had to take. She didn't see any other alternative, so she turned about abruptly, heading across the lawn to the path leading to the farm. Her heart was in her throat when she reached the Hopkinses' old stone house and stood outside the door, working up the courage to knock.

"Come on in," said Hopp, with a big smile when he opened the door. "We don't get too many visitors anymore, do we, Susan?"

"Always the joker," said Susan, greeting Lucy. She was seated at the kitchen table along with Will and Brad, gathered around a Scrabble board. A glowing kerosene lantern hung from the ceiling, illuminating the cozy room where the small windows, and the roof's overhang, didn't allow much outside light to enter. It was a homey scene right out of a Norman Rockwell painting. "What brings you here?"

Lucy hesitated, unwilling to show her hand so soon. Better to proceed cautiously, she decided, feeling things out. "Oh, cabin fever, I guess."

"In that case you've come to the wrong place," said Will, a mischievous glint in his eye. "You've exchanged Scott's mansion for our humble home."

"Believe me, that mansion feels pretty claustrophobic right now," said Lucy, casually leaning against the kitchen counter.

"Pull up a chair," invited Brad, with an easy smile. "Do you play?"

"I'm not in the mood," said Lucy. "But

carry on. I'll watch, if you don't mind."

"As long as you don't coach," said Will, fetching a chair from the small, crowded living room. "We take the game pretty seriously."

Lucy seated herself and watched, impressed as Susan racked up a sizable score with *exquisite,* only to be topped by Will, who got a triple-word score simply by adding *l* and *y.* It certainly wasn't logical, she was sure somewhere there was a Scrabble-playing serial killer, but witnessing the game and the family members' humorous interactions with each other had given her the reassurance she needed.

"I didn't come here to watch you play Scrabble," she finally confessed. "I came because I suspect you have a marine radio."

"I thought you were up to something," said Hopp, with a satisfied smirk.

"Well, do you?" asked Lucy. "Do you have a radio?"

"What if we do?" asked Brad, in a challenging tone.

"Not that he's saying we do," added Will, cagily.

By now, Lucy was pretty sure the family did have a radio. The trick was to convince them to use it. "To call for help, of course. We've got to find those boys."

"The boys are long gone," said Susan, sadly. "They're not on the island, they were taken by the sea."

Lucy thought she was probably right; she'd covered plenty of stories where one person got in trouble in the water and another jumped in, trying to help, and both ended up drowning. But she wasn't ready to admit it.

She was alone in that, however. The others were all nodding sadly, agreeing with Susan.

"And if we had a radio, and used it, and Scott found out, he'd kick us off the island," said Will.

"For sure," added Susan, with a curt nod.

"Scott's not well," said Lucy. "He's behaving strangely and I'm afraid he's going to do something desperate that will put us all in danger. Lily's terrified, and so is Taylor. They think he's lost touch with reality."

"Breaking news! Hold the presses!" scoffed Brad.

"First clue was when he decided it would be a good idea to stop the clock and go back to the nineteenth century," said Will.

"He's been heading off the rails for some time now," said Hopp, scratching his beard.

"Well, then we have to do something, for his sake, as well as our own," insisted Lucy.

"He's dangerous. Lily says he has guns, she fears he's going to refuse to allow any sort of official investigation on the island."

"That's ridiculous," scoffed Susan. "Parker's death was unattended. There has to be an investigation to determine the cause of death. He can't stop it."

"Lily says he might very well try. She even fears *he* might have killed the twins, acting on some delusion or something."

"That's flat-out ridiculous," said Brad.

"I'm not so sure, Brad," said Will. "Remember that time he flipped because you got arrested over in the Cove, that time you had a few too many beers and borrowed Nate Sparrow's car? I thought he was going to kill you; he tried to throw you overboard. Said he didn't want police sniffing around, he had some crazy idea the FBI would get involved because you were working for him. We had the devil of a time convincing him you were just going to pay a fine and lose your license for six months."

"It sounds like he's desperate to hide something," said Lucy. "Probably some illegal business thing. Maybe money laundering, off-shore bank accounts, something like that."

"And Lily thinks he'd kill his children over it?" Susan was doubtful.

"We don't know how big the secret is," said Brad.

"Maybe the kids are the secret," said Will. "Maybe he's abused them and is afraid they'll tell."

"Or maybe he thinks in some deluded way that he's protecting his family, or what's left of it," said Lucy.

"Well, there's one thing I know for sure," said Will, "and that's that he don't give a dang about us. We're screwed no matter what. We're gonna have to leave the island sooner or later, and I'd rather leave on my feet than feet first, if you get my meaning."

They did. It was like watching instant pudding solidify. It started as goopy liquid and after a few stirs, presto chango, you had thick, creamy pudding. One minute the various members of the family held diverse opinions; then they all came together. "Okay," said Hopp. "We're gonna send out an SOS. Agreed?"

They all nodded. Then Hopp got to his feet and opened the kitchen door. "This way," he said, inviting Lucy to follow him.

"You want to do the honors?" asked Hopp, speaking to Will.

"Sure thing." Will got to his feet and the three of them left together, walking a short distance through the fading light to a shed that was overgrown with a wisteria vine. It was dark inside the shed, and Will switched on a powerful, battery-powered lamp and exclaimed, "Crap!"

He stepped aside and Lucy saw several burst bags of top soil, and beneath the scattered mess the smashed remains of the radio.

"Can you fix it?" she asked.

Will was brushing away the dirt and picking through the pieces, shaking his head. "We're done for," he said.

"Well," said Hopp, slapping his hands against his thighs, "we knew that anyways."

CHAPTER FOURTEEN

Lucy picked up one of the scattered electrical components, a bit of circuit board, and stared at it. Oddly enough, although the destruction was catastrophic, she found she wasn't the least bit surprised. Whoever was behind all this mischief had been one step ahead of everyone the whole time: killing Parker, wrecking the boats, kidnapping the boys, and now, destroying the island's only radio. "Do you have any idea when this could have happened?" she asked.

Hopp shook his head. "We've been so busy, what with looking for the boys and all, I haven't had any reason to go into the shed."

"I don't suppose you bother to lock it," said Lucy.

"Up 'til now there was no need," said Will. "We thought we could trust everybody on the island."

For a moment, Lucy thought he was

implying that she was the troublemaker, since she was the only newcomer, and she was quick to defend herself. "If you think I . . ."

Hopp was quick to smooth things over. "Nobody thinks you had anything to do with any of this," he said, patting her shoulder. "But it is true that we never had any violence on the island until now."

"Scott brought it with him," said Will, kicking the stack of bagged topsoil. "And he brought those two city slickers. I dunno what they think they're doing here."

"Nuthin' good, I warrant," said Hopp. "Let's go back to the house. We need to come up with a plan. The ferry's due day after tomorrow, and we've gotta make sure it gets here and there's no, uh, complications."

He hoisted the lamp and led the way through the now-dark, scrappy little yard to the house, where Susan immediately sensed something was wrong. "Don't tell me . . ." she said, looking up as they entered.

"Yup, radio was smashed to smithereens," said Hopp, turning off his lamp and setting it on a handy shelf by the door.

"How can that be? Nobody but us knew about the radio," she said.

Lucy was busy putting two and two together. Taylor had been trying to call for help for days on her cell phone, and she had also been spending a lot of time with Brad. She might well have asked him if the family had a radio, and even if he denied it, might have grown suspicious. But, she wondered, should she say something?

"Anybody might have guessed," said Brad, as if reading her thoughts and deciding to put up a defense.

Will wasn't about to fall for it. "Like your little cutie?" he demanded.

Brad was all innocence. "Who do you mean?" he demanded, lowering his chin and glowering at his brother.

Will wasn't about to back down. "Taylor, of course," he said, flexing his hands. "You two have been thick as thieves."

For a moment it looked as if the two brothers were going to come to blows, but then Brad shrugged and sat down. "She asked, but I never told her. It made her pretty mad."

Lucy remembered the raised voices she'd heard earlier in the day, when they were searching the old village. So that's what they'd been arguing about.

"She even accused us of taking the twins; she said we wanted to get back at her father for buying the island," continued Brad, shaking his head. "She got all dramatic, begged me to tell her where we'd hidden them."

"As if," said Susan, clearly hurt by the accusation. "As if any one of us would harm a hair of those darling boys' heads."

"Pay no mind," said Hopp, patting her on the shoulder. "I know you're more of a mother to those tykes than their own mother."

Lucy thought of the endless plates of cookies and glasses of milk Susan put out for the boys, who were always welcome in the kitchen. "It's true," she said. "You spent a lot of time with them, did you get any sense of . . . I don't know, anything at all that would help us find them?"

Susan bit her lip and seemed to be struggling with her conscience. "I don't hold with gossip," she said.

"C'mon, Ma. It's no secret. The Newmans are not a happy family," said Brad.

She gave her son a crooked little smile. "You're right. It was a lot of pretend, all that business about everyone loving to be on the island. The girls hated the island, and they hated their father for making them be there. They resented Lily and called her 'the evil stepmother' behind her back, and

Lily thought they were spoiled and useless brats."

"But Scott gave the girls jobs in his company, important jobs," said Lucy.

"Lily told me those were just empty titles, that they didn't really do anything except collect big paychecks."

Lucy had suspected as much, but still found Susan's version of events upsetting. She, too, had fallen for the fantasy and wanted to believe the island was a special, protected place that nurtured a perfect family. "And what about the boys?" she asked. "They were happy here, weren't they?"

Susan shook her head. "They missed their friends and their video games, and they knew things weren't right. Daddy was drinking too much and Mommy was too distracted to pay attention to them and the girls were mean to them."

"Mean? How?"

"Oh, you know. Sibling stuff. Called them 'little worms' and threatened them, warning them to mind their own business or else."

Lucy nodded, comparing the Newmans to her own family and thinking it all sounded pretty familiar. Except more so, which she thought was probably the result of taking a pretty typical family and isolating them on an island with none of the modern conveniences they were used to. And none of it seemed an adequate explanation for the tragic events that were besetting the family.

"Getting back to the matter of the ferry," said Hopp, redirecting the conversation. "We need to make sure we can get some help from the authorities, whether Scott wants it or not. Anybody got any ideas?"

"I think we need to spread out, so we're not any easy target," said Brad.

"No good. That way we could get picked off, one by one," countered Will.

"Maybe stage some sort of distraction?" suggested Lucy.

"That's a good idea," said Hopp. "Something to draw attention away from the ferry."

"Who exactly are we defending ourselves against?" asked Susan. "I think that's the real question."

"It's Scott," said Hopp. "He's been our enemy since day one."

"Aided and abetted by Ben-ee-th-io and Volfgang," said Will, attempting foreign accents for the names. "Those two are nothing but trouble."

Lucy noticed from their little nods that the whole family seemed to agree with him, and she certainly wasn't about to argue with them, but she didn't think Wolf and Ben had anything to do with the terrible events on the island. After talking with each of the guys, she'd gotten the distinct impression that they both thought coming to the island was a big mistake and they were eager to get away. Wolf missed his girlfriend in Germany, and Ben longed to return to his old neighborhood in Brooklyn. No, she thought, it was Hopp who was on the right track.

It had to be Scott. He was the loose cannon, the one with paranoid delusions fueled by alcohol. Nobody else could be causing so much mayhem. No rational person would act like that. And maybe he wasn't even aware of what he was doing, maybe he'd done it all while in some altered state? Maybe he had multiple personalities, and the good Scott didn't know what the bad Scott did. She sighed, realizing that it was getting late and she had to go back to the house. "Well," she began, "I guess I better be going."

"Be careful," said Hopp. "It's dark now, you know."

"Do you want one of the boys to go with you?" offered Susan.

"Oh, no, I'll be fine," said Lucy, which was her usual automatic response to anything that might cause anyone other than herself an inconvenience. She pulled the little flashlight out of her pocket. "Always prepared, that's me," she said, waving it.

"Well, watch your step," said Hopp.

"See you in the morning," she said, stepping outside into the dark and making out the ghostly shadow of the moon. It was not enough light to see by, so she flicked on the flashlight. "Spo-o-oky," she said, under her breath, imitating one of her grandson Patrick's cute expressions, which he'd picked up one Halloween years ago, when he was only three, and soon abandoned. The family, however, had adopted it and continued to use it.

The mini-flash cast a surprisingly powerful beam of light for its size, and she found the path quite easily, but she didn't appreciate seeing the little creatures of the night, which included some rather large spiders, fleeing back into the darkness. Moths fluttered about her and bats flew overhead, sometimes zooming too close for comfort before darting away, and when she entered the little patch of woods between the meadow and the lawn, she heard strange rustlings in the pine needle and leaf litter that covered the forest floor. She wondered if the lamp was attracting all this wildlife and decided to try turning it off and relying on the faint moonlight that penetrated the fog. She stood there, waiting for her eyes to adjust, when she distinctly heard a twig snap.

The sudden noise made her heart leap in her chest and she let out an involuntary gasp. *Nothing to worry about,* she told herself. *Probably just some animal.* She took a deep breath and forced herself to move, continuing along the path, all the time trying to figure out what island animal was large enough to snap a twig. A good-sized twig, she guessed, from the loudness of the snap. Although, she reasoned, it was very quiet on the island at night, you might even say the silence was overwhelming, so even a little noise seemed quite loud. It was probably nothing larger than a raccoon. Not that she was that keen about raccoons, who could be quite nasty and aggressive if provoked. *Okay, raccoons, let's just agree to get along. I won't bother you, you don't bother me.*

That's when she heard a thud, followed by heavy breathing. *Not a raccoon.* She flicked the lamp back on and quickened her pace, only to realize that she wasn't on the path at all. She must have wandered off the path and into the thickly wooded forest after she'd turned off the lamp. *Stupid. Stupid.*

Bad idea. She cast the lamp about, hoping to find the path, but all she saw were dark shapes and shadows that loomed all around her. It seemed as if she was surrounded by all the terrifying ghouls and goblins of fairy tale nights: witches, hideous monsters, ogres, and trolls.

Get a grip. She cast her eyes skyward, hoping to catch sight of the Big Dipper and its companion, the North Star, but there were no stars to be seen, only the dimmest moon. It had been on her left, when she noticed it earlier, so she decided that if she kept moving in the same direction, with the moon always on her left, she would eventually reach the mansion. That, however, was not always possible because she encountered thick stands of bushes, thorny vines, and large boulders that she had to go around. It wasn't long before she was hopelessly confused, and began to panic. Her breath was coming in short, ragged gasps, and sweat was running down her back, despite the cool night. Confronted by a tangle of brambles, she stopped and tried to calm herself and catch her breath.

She could hear the sea roaring and waves crashing, which meant she must have gotten turned around and gone in the wrong direction, toward the back of the island. She rotated slowly, trying to pinpoint the direction that the sound was coming from, but instead heard heavy footfalls coming toward her. She immediately flicked off the lamp, which made her an obvious target, and started to run, circling the thicket in desperate hope of finding a clear way forward. She heard the thuds behind her, following her, and turned her head to see, only to slam into a tree.

"Stop!" ordered a masculine voice. "Identify yourself."

Stunned by the impact with the tree, Lucy knew the jig was up, she was trapped. Voice shaking with fear, she identified herself. "It's me. Lucy."

"You shouldn't be out here in the dark, Lucy." The figure stepped closer and Lucy realized her pursuer was Scott.

"Oh, you scared me," said Lucy, both relieved and cautious. What was he doing out in the night? And more importantly, could she trust him?

"Turn on your lamp," he said.

Lucy obeyed, and he stepped forward into the circle of light.

Seeing him, Lucy gasped. Scott was dressed entirely in black and had night-vision goggles flipped up, attached to some sort of helmet, and he'd blackened his face.

Most disturbingly, he was carrying what looked to Lucy to be an assault rifle.

"What are you doing out here?" he demanded.

"I was out for a walk and got lost," said Lucy.

"You were coming from the farm," he said. "I saw you. What were you doing there?"

Lucy wasn't about to admit she'd gone hoping the Hopkinses had a radio. "I stopped in for directions," she said, hoping it sounded plausible.

"I'm surprised they let you leave on your own, since you were obviously lost. One of them should have guided you back."

"They offered, but I figured I'd be fine, following the path."

"It's confusing out here, it's easy enough to get lost during the day."

"Well, I'm glad you found me," said Lucy, hoping she'd have no reason to change her mind. "Do you patrol the island every night?" It seemed impossible, considering how he'd passed out after dinner. But maybe he'd gotten a second wind, fueled by alcohol and paranoia.

"Have been, since Parker's death."

"Have you found any intruders?" asked Lucy.

"Not yet," he replied, "but I know they're here."

"How do you know?"

"Footprints. Markings on the trees, that's how they signal to each other. Slashes, scratches. They've got their own signs; I don't know what they mean, but they're there."

"I believe you," said Lucy, thinking it best to agree with him. "Do you have any idea who they are and why they want to hurt you?"

"Oh, yeah. Big oil hates me, they'd do anything to shut me up. The government, too. Do you know the government is owned lock, stock, and barrel by the fossil fuel industry? True fact: Carbon emissions are going up because they're burning more coal. If we don't stop them, they'll kill the planet."

"No wonder you're concerned," said Lucy, nodding along. "Do you think you could show me the way back to the house?"

"I'll take you. Don't want you to end up like Parker, or to disappear, like the boys."

"Have you found any sign of them?" asked Lucy, as she followed in Scott's combat-booted footsteps.

"Not yet. I expect I'll get a ransom demand soon. Not money, they don't want my money. They'll want me to eat crow. I'll have to issue a statement, maybe admit to some false crime or something. I'm not sure I'll do it."

"Not even to save your boys?"

"Once I've got the ransom demand, I'll know who I'm up against. I might be able to launch a counterattack."

"So you've got a plan," said Lucy, heartened to see they'd reached the path. Spotting a broken tree she recognized, she knew she wasn't far from the house, and relative safety.

"They shouldn't mess with me," he said. "They don't know what they're up against. I've even got rocket launchers."

Good Lord, thought Lucy, fearing he might actually use one to take out the ferry. "I sure hope it doesn't come to that," she said, finally stepping out onto the lawn. The mansion was a dark, shadowy shape in the distance, and only a few windows were still alight.

"Here you are," he said. "Safe and sound. Don't try this again, don't go out at night. It's not safe."

"I won't go out," promised Lucy. "I realize it's dangerous."

But the danger, she thought, as she climbed the porch steps, was not from

Scott's imaginary invaders. It was Scott who was dangerous.

CHAPTER FIFTEEN

Lucy stripped off her clothes, climbed into bed and pulled the covers up to her chin, and immediately fell asleep. She slept right through the night and woke refreshed, buoyed with the knowledge that there was only one more day to get through before the ferry would arrive. It was due at eleven the next morning, and Lucy planned to get on it no matter what.

Still lying in bed, Lucy stretched her legs, which had tightened after the previous day's workout. She'd been on her feet for the entire day, she remembered, first searching for the boys and then walking out to the Hopkins homestead, losing her way on the hike home, followed by her frightening encounter with Scott. Every muscle in her body protested when she got out of bed, and a peek in the mirror revealed several nasty scratches on her face, reminders of her close encounter with that tree. It had been quite a night, she decided, as she headed for the bathroom.

Meeting Scott had been the worst part, she thought, as she splashed water on her face. That had been truly frightening, as well as enlightening. She was now absolutely convinced that Scott was completely detached from reality, and was amazed by the fact that it had taken so long for her to recognize it. Although, she supposed, he must have been able to fool numerous investors, members of his company's board of directors, and even scores of media interviewers who'd eagerly swallowed his nonsense and reported what they termed his "unique insights."

She'd had enough, she decided, as she went back to her room to dress. One more day, that was it. She was horrified by Parker's death, her heart went out to Lily and the two little boys, but in truth she was only an accidental bystander. She had come to the island as a visitor to report on Scott's efforts to create a pollution-free, historically accurate environment for his family and instead had witnessed a series of tragedies. No question the Newman family's troubles would make a terrific story, a first witness account, but it truly had nothing to do with her. Professional detachment was the order of the day, necessary to avoid being consumed by needless and pointless emotional turmoil. She remembered what her editor, Ted, had told her when she was assigned to interview surviving family members for her first obituary, which happened to be for an eight-year-old boy who was hit by a car while riding his bicycle: "You've got to remain objective, he's not your little kid."

Well, Parker wasn't her daughter, her three daughters were alive and well. Admittedly, one in particular, Zoe, definitely required some tactful, motherly attention as she was making a big mistake by falling for that awful Mike guy. And Walter and Fred weren't her sons, or grandsons, either. Toby and Patrick were just fine, thank you, off in Alaska, where they'd recently taken up soccer as a father-son activity.

So that was it, she concluded, tying her shoelaces and heading downstairs for some breakfast. She was willing to help, she'd do all she could for the Newmans, but her main priority was staying safe so she could get on that ferry tomorrow and sail away home, away from this cursed island.

All her resolve faded, however, as soon as she entered the kitchen and saw Taylor sitting alone at the table, staring into a cup of coffee. "It's so quiet without the boys," she said, looking up, with dark circles under her reddened eyes. She looked, thought Lucy, as if she'd been crying all night.

"It sure is," said Lucy, taking a cup off the shelf and filling it from the coffeepot on the stove. "Where is everybody? Susan's usually here by now."

"Hopp came by earlier and left a note saying her sciatica was acting up and she'd try to come in later."

"I didn't know she had sciatica," said Lucy, who'd seen no sign that Susan was ailing when she was at the house last night. She wondered if the sciatica was a sort of dishpan diarrhea, a fake excuse so Susan could stay away from the uneasy situation at the mansion.

"Me either," said Taylor. "Hopp got the stove going and made coffee, but that was all. I guess we'll have to fend for ourselves. Do you want eggs or something?" She continued, sounding less confident, "I guess we can figure out how to use the stove."

"No, I'll just have some cold cereal." Lucy went in the pantry, where she found several boxes and chose Raisin Bran. "Do you want some?" she asked, filling a bowl and adding milk from the pitcher of fresh, but warm goat's milk on the counter. The icebox hadn't had fresh ice since Parker's body was placed in the icehouse.

"No, I'm not hungry," said Taylor, studying her. "What happened to your face?"

"I got in a fight with a tree," said Lucy.

"Well, it looks like the tree won," said Taylor, with a half smile. "Do you want to come out with me today to see the puffins? I've been neglecting the study."

"Because of your ankle?" asked Lucy.

Taylor took a swallow of coffee, carefully replacing her cup on its saucer. "That, and everything else. It's much better now, but I could sure use some help, now that Parker's gone."

Lucy considered Taylor's offer. It was tempting, because it would fill some of the twenty-seven or so hours that remained until the ferry came, and it would get her out of the house. That, however, was the rub. As much as she would have liked to get outside, away from the oppressive atmosphere in the house, she suspected it wasn't a good idea. After last night's misadventure she was convinced it was dangerous out there, and even though she didn't think Taylor posed any threat to her safety, she wasn't about to risk it. Parker had fallen to her death from the puffin nesting ground, and Lucy knew it was treacherous, that a wrong step onto unstable ground could be fatal.

247

Better safe than sorry, she decided.

"Thanks, but no thanks," she told Taylor. "I'm really tired, I think I might be coming down with something."

"Sciatica?" inquired Taylor in a rather sarcastic tone.

So Taylor had her doubts about Susan, too, thought Lucy. "No, more like flu," she said in a serious tone. "A lot of aches and pains," she added, truthfully, since she did have a lot of tired muscles today. "I could use some rest, maybe fight it off."

"The fresh air might do you good," suggested Taylor, pressing the issue.

Lucy wondered if Taylor, too, was hesitant to go out alone. Maybe she should go with her, a little exercise and fresh air wouldn't kill her, would it? Lucy was about to agree, when Taylor caught her eye.

"I'd really like some company," she said in a coaxing tone. "It's times like this," she added, her voice breaking, "that I really miss my sister."

That's when alarm bells went off in Lucy's head, something a bit off about Taylor, and she smiled sadly. "Honestly, I'd love to go, but I just don't feel up to it."

"Okay," said Taylor, admitting defeat with a shrug. "I'm going anyway. It's something to do, and I'll keep an eye out for any sign of the twins."

"Good idea," said Lucy, picking up her spoon and digging into her warm, soggy Raisin Bran.

That was weird, she thought, as Taylor gathered her puffin study gear and headed out the door. Why on earth did she have that reaction, that sudden aversion to being alone with Taylor? It was the island, the house, the entire situation, she decided, scooping up another spoonful of cereal. It was getting to her.

After washing up the breakfast things, Lucy wandered into the living room, looking for something to read. No one was there, which came as a relief, and she studied the tall bookshelf looking for something light, maybe a book of short stories. Oddly enough, however, the shelves were filled with musty old volumes by Dickens and Scott, along with the collected poems of Longfellow and Edgar Guest. The selection reminded her of the books passed down from her great-grandfather, which her mother had boxed up and stored in the attic, and which were eventually thrown out when she moved into assisted living.

At least she'd get a chuckle from Edgar Guest, she decided, pulling out the volume and settling down on one of the couches.

The book smelled musty, but she had to admit the one about mother's checkbook was pretty funny, albeit sexist and terribly dated. Who even wrote checks anymore?

She was idly turning the pages when a fragile bit of browned old newsprint fell into her lap. She snatched it up eagerly, hoping it was some sort of clue, but found it was only an advertisement from T.T. Parris & Son, Quality Provisions offering weekly island delivery by motor launch in the months of July and August. "Reliable and Honest" promised the ad, which made Lucy smile. Island life, it seemed, had become a lot more difficult.

She was sitting there, imagining old times on the island, when ladies in puffy-sleeved long dresses, holding parasols to protect their complexions from the damaging rays of the sun, strolled across the lawn to watch T.T. Parris's little launch bring the week's groceries, when Lily drifted into the room. As always, she was dressed in fluttery bits of chiffon, but today she hadn't bothered to arrange her hair or apply her usual careful makeup. Without moisturizer her skin looked crepey and dry, her lips were chapped, and her eyes had sunk into their sockets.

Lily perched lightly on the edge of the opposite sofa, then hopped up and went to the window, looking out. "I can't seem to settle," she said with a sigh. "All I can think about are my boys. It's gotten so I actually hope they've died, so they're not suffering, trapped under some fallen tree or something. Or worse, held by kidnappers."

"Have you heard something? Last night Scott was talking about possibly receiving a ransom note," said Lucy.

Lily turned away from the window, the sun backlighting her messy hair, giving her a halo, and Lucy thought she looked like a saint in a Pre-Raphaelite painting. "I don't think so," she said, wringing her hands. "How would it be delivered? And even if it was, I'm not sure Scott would tell me." She pressed her lips together. "He's on his own trip, you know?"

"I know," said Lucy.

"He's out searching again today. He's rounded up all the men. They're going to beat the bushes, look under every rock, he's determined to find . . ." Her voice trailed off and she brushed away tears. " 'Some clue,' that's what he said, but after all this time . . ."

Some sort of distraction was called for, decided Lucy, setting the book aside and getting up. "Have you eaten anything today?" she asked.

"Oh, I couldn't."

"Well, let's try a cup of tea," said Lucy, taking Lily's arm and leading her to the kitchen.

Easier said than done, Lucy discovered, staring at the huge black range, which was now barely warm. Nothing ventured, nothing gained, she decided. It was time to show this monster who was boss. She opened a few doors, found the fire box, and shoveled in a few pieces of wood, wondering exactly why Scott considered a smoky wood fire to be good for the environment. She noticed an iron rod hanging on a nearby hook and used it to give the wood a poke or two and, amazingly enough, the fire flickered into life and she closed the door. A circular lid on the top of the range was directly above the fire box, so she put the half-full kettle there. Only half-full, so it would come to a boil faster. Then she popped a couple of tea bags into a teapot and rummaged through the various tins on the counter until she found one containing the last of the molasses cookies. She put them on a plate, which she set on the table in front of Lily.

"Shouldn't be long," said Lucy.

"You're amazing," said Lily. "I wouldn't have the first idea how to work that thing."

"Well, let's not count our chickens before they've hatched," said Lucy. "It's not boiling yet."

It was then that they heard the men outside, ringing bells and calling the boys' names, and Lily practically jumped out of her seat. "I'll go mad," she said, her eyes widening.

Lucy cast about desperately for a distraction and ended up asking her about Taylor and Parker. "It must have been odd, being stepmother to two young women," she said, immediately wishing she could bite her tongue off. What a gaffe! Why didn't she ever think before she spoke? But much to her surprise, Lily wasn't the least bit offended.

"Well, they were in their teens when Scott and I married, so you can imagine, it was pretty challenging. I was only in my late twenties then and I knew I couldn't really be a mother to them, so I tried instead to be a kind aunt, or maybe an older sister. I took them for facials and shopping, I pretty much spoiled the hell out of them."

The kettle was finally actually steaming, so Lucy got up and filled the teapot. Then she brought a couple of cups to the table, followed by the teapot and sugar bowl. "Do you take milk?" she asked.

"Oh, no," said Lily, smiling serenely, apparently remembering happy days in Nordstrom and Neiman Marcus. "Fortunately, they weren't overweight or ugly or anything like that, and it was lots of fun to find cute things for them to wear."

Lucy wasn't sure she was buying Lily's reminiscences. She was remembering Susan's claim that the girls called Lily an evil stepmother, and that Lily returned the favor by calling the girls spoiled brats.

"That's very unusual, I think," said Lucy, pouring the tea. "You'd expect a certain amount of resentment."

"Well, nobody's perfect," said Lily, picking up a cookie and nibbling at the edge. "But I tried and I think we got along pretty well." She took another nibble, and swallowed. "I do feel terrible about Parker. I thought that was the worst thing that could happen, but I was wrong."

"Here, have some tea," said Lucy, sliding the cup and saucer across the table. "I put a little sugar in, just a touch. It will do you good." In actuality, she'd dumped in a heaping spoonful.

"Scott must be very upset at losing Parker," said Lucy, feeling as if she were pushing the envelope. "He'd just made her a partner, didn't he?"

Lily stirred her tea, then shrugged. "I don't really pay attention to Scott's business affairs. He's right brain and I'm left, if you know what I mean. When this is over, well . . ."

Lucy had a sudden insight. Lily was hanging on by a thread, and she'd already decided her marriage was over. "You'll go back to singing?" said Lucy.

Lily nodded. "Yes, I really miss it. And I was good. I got on the charts a couple of times. And if I'm going to do it, I can't wait. I'm not getting any younger." She picked up her cookie and took a tiny bite, following it by a sip of tea. Setting her cup back down on its saucer, she smiled. "That's what I'm going to do."

"Good for you," said Lucy, as the men moved away from the house and the shouts and clanging bells grew fainter.

"You know," added Lily, "that song Eric Clapton wrote about meeting his little boy in heaven, after the child fell to his death from an open window in his mother's New York apartment, you know that song?"

"I do," said Lucy, figuring everybody knew that song.

"Well, it was a big hit."

Oh, my, thought Lucy. Lily apparently had a mercenary streak, and wasn't nearly as fragile as she appeared. Then, for a fleeting moment, Lucy wondered if Lily was behind the boys' disappearance, or Parker's death. No, oh, no, she decided. That was too awful to even contemplate.

"I think that song must have made Eric Clapton a lot of money," said Lily.

"I think he donated it to charity," said Lucy.

Lily picked up her cookie, took another tiny bite, and stared out the window over the sink. Lucy thought she would have given almost anything to be able to read her mind at that moment, then reconsidered. She really didn't want to go there.

Chapter Sixteen

After Lily wandered into the living room and began strumming on her guitar, Lucy went out on the porch. Standing there, she noticed the fog seemed less dense than it had been and was pierced by rays of weak sunlight. The air felt lighter and cooler, too, which was an encouraging sign. Perhaps tomorrow would be clear.

She debated joining the men in their search for the boys, but her sore and aching muscles insisted that wasn't a good idea. Maybe later, she decided guiltily, sitting down on one of the comfy wicker armchairs and picking up one of the old magazines from the pile on the adjacent table. It was *The New Yorker,* swollen from the humidity and double in size, and although the stories were outdated, the cartoons were still funny. She flipped through it, occasionally chuckling, soon reaching the last page. There she found the cartoon contest, which featured a drawing without a caption and invited readers to send in their suggestions.

Much to her amusement, the drawing pictured two concerned parents standing by the front door, watching their daughter ride off on a motorcycle with a bearded and tattooed Hells Angel. She could imagine what the parents' reaction might be, and plenty of comments came to mind, but none of them were funny.

Her thoughts turned to Zoe's relationship with Mike Snider, which she realized she hadn't given much thought while on the island. No wonder, since she'd been so overwhelmed by the recent events, but now she was about to leave and would have to deal with the Mike question when she got home. Or would she? Maybe Zoe had come to her senses and sent him packing.

Remembering Zoe's impassioned defense of her boyfriend, and the torrid embraces she'd witnessed, Lucy thought that was unlikely. She shook her head, wondering what on earth Zoe found so attractive about Mike. He was scruffy and dirty, he was lazy and rude, and it was really hard to imagine why Zoe found him so desirable. Lucy found him absolutely repellent and physically repulsive; she found herself reaching for the Febreze spray in order to freshen the sofa whenever he vacated it.

However, she reminded herself, it wasn't Mike's physical attractiveness that should concern her. It was the potential emotional damage he was likely to inflict on lovestruck Zoe. She knew that her youngest daughter was relatively naïve, and hadn't had a serious boyfriend until now. Mike was the first, though calling him serious was probably not accurate. Zoe was head over heels, but Mike didn't really seem that taken with Zoe. He seemed a lot more interested in the Stone family's refrigerator and the expensive cable TV subscription that Bill insisted upon, featuring every sport known to mankind. She'd even stumbled on the curling channel while searching for HGTV.

She thought grimly that her mother, rest her soul, would have termed Mike a lounge lizard, but she thought couch potato was closer to the truth. For once installed on the family's sectional, he expected Zoe to supply all his needs, whether it be for a cold beer or some heavy petting. She assumed the pair hadn't stopped at heavy petting, but hoped it hadn't happened on her upholstered furniture. And, please God, she added, praying they used a condom.

It was then the thought struck her: What if Parker was pregnant? In her years as a reporter she'd covered several stories involving missing young women who had turned up dead, and pregnant. The minister who'd fallen for the pretty young chorister's trilling amens couldn't face being exposed as a sinner, the professor who'd so admired his graduate student's insights into Emily Dickinson's poetry wasn't about to risk his marriage, and the assistant manager at the big box store wasn't about to allow a paternity claim to derail his rising career.

Getting pregnant was dangerous for a young woman, especially if she was foolish enough to present her lover with an ultimatum. Demands like "Marry me or else," or even "give me money for an abortion" often backfired, only to end with the cadaver-sniffing dog making a gruesome discovery. Was that what happened to Parker?

Lucy considered each of the men on the island, wondering if one of them had an intimate relationship with Parker, and whether a pregnancy would have been disastrous for him. She dismissed Brad and Will immediately, not because she didn't think either was capable of the crime, but because they knew the tides intimately and would have timed the murder so that the body would have been carried out to sea. The same went for Hopp, who was also rather old for romance. Then again, from what she'd read in the advice columns, men didn't seem to lose their libido and remained sexually active quite late in life, which wasn't always appreciated by their postmenopausal wives.

What about Ben and Wolf? Wolf claimed he had a girlfriend in Germany, and said he wouldn't dream of cheating on her. Could he be believed? Lucy had originally thought so, but now she wondered. If he had fathered a child with Parker and she refused to have an abortion, even if she insisted she wouldn't expect anything from him, he might have felt threatened. The fact that he had fathered a child would have hung over him and could have come up sooner or later, presenting him with an awkward situation. A situation that could be avoided by giving Parker a little shove and sending her over the cliff, where he might wrongly have assumed the sea would carry her body away.

And then there was Ben, who claimed he wanted nothing more than to return to his beloved Brooklyn. He had said he viewed both Parker and Taylor as trouble, and had been determined to stay clear of them, but perhaps that was something he realized after the fact. Lucy had only seen Parker in action, briefly, at the party, and again that first night on the island, but she was certainly attractive and appealing. Any man, especially a young and healthy one like Ben, would need a great deal of resolve to resist her if she came on to him.

Lucy's thoughts were interrupted by the clatter of pots, and she guessed that Susan was feeling better and had come to make lunch. She put her suspicions aside, deciding that was really all they were, and got up to see if Susan needed any help.

When she entered the kitchen she found Susan emptying the ice box and tossing everything into a giant stock pot set in the kitchen sink. "There's no more ice and we sure can't get any, so we've got to use it all up before it's too far gone," she said, sniffing a plate of chicken pieces and deciding they were all right. "In they go!" she said, adding them to the pot, which she began filling with water.

"Soup for dinner?" asked Lucy.

"Yup, I'll use the stock and make a minestrone, there's a lot of baby veggies in the garden."

"Sounds good," said Lucy. "How's your sciatica?"

"Better. I took some aspirin and did my exercises. I'd been neglecting them, what with everything, and when I do that it catches up with me." She gave the faucet a twist, turning it off, and winced. "Would you mind lifting the pot for me and setting it on the stove?"

"No problem," said Lucy, easily completing the task. "So what's the plan for tomorrow?"

Susan shrugged. "Hopp says he's working on it, that's all he'll say, so I figure he hasn't really come up with a plan yet."

"Any new developments?" asked Lucy. "I know Scott's got the men out searching for the boys."

"They're not going to find them," said Susan, easing herself into one of the kitchen chairs. "I had a dream last night, real vivid it was, too. About the boys."

Lucy wasn't impressed. "And that's how you know they're gone?"

Susan nodded. "I don't often dream, but when I do, it's a message."

"From who?"

Susan shrugged, then grimaced with pain. "Them that went before."

"And what did them have to say?" asked Lucy.

"They said not to worry about the little ones, they're coming to a better place."

"But they're only coming?" Lucy's hopes rose. "That means they're still alive."

"Not necessarily. The spirits kind of wander about for a bit, as I understand it, before they settle into the better place."

Lucy got up to stir the pot and skim off the scum that was beginning to form as the contents of the pot started to simmer. "Maybe it wasn't them that went before at all, maybe it was indigestion, or sciatica."

Susan was philosophical. "I did take some sleeping stuff, but the way I see it, that sort of thing just opens the channels so the spirits can be heard."

Lucy gazed out the window, where she saw a hummingbird dart by, pausing by a hanging plant. "What's that quote? 'Hope is the thing with feathers?' Maybe that hummer is a sign that we shouldn't give up hope, how about that?"

"Each to her own," said Susan, groaning a bit as she rose from her chair. "I guess I'll mix up some biscuits for lunch. We're out of bread and there isn't time to make yeast bread."

"I'll do it," offered Lucy.

"Thanks. While you do the biscuits, I'll get the dough started for bread, so we'll have it for the next few days."

That's right, thought Lucy, as she sifted flour into a bowl. She was going to leave tomorrow, but Susan and the others weren't so lucky. They had to stay on the island and face the consequences of the inevitable official investigation. If things were bad now, it was only going to get worse. And, she thought, with a shiver of fear, whoever was behind all the trouble must certainly be getting very anxious, and therefore dangerous.

She was pounding away at her biscuit dough with the rolling pin when Susan spoke up. "You don't have to beat them into submission, you know. They're just biscuits."

"Oh, right," said Lucy, remembering her mother's admonitions about tender hands making tender biscuits.

When she had filled two baking sheets with the biscuits and slid them into the oven, it occurred to her that they looked a lot like hockey pucks. In fact, she remembered Toby once taking some stale biscuits and using them for that very purpose. "If they're too tough, the boys can use them for hockey practice," she said, momentarily forgetting that the twins were still missing. Suddenly overcome, she collapsed on a chair and started to cry.

"No matter," said Susan, patting her shoulder. "I forget sometimes, too. I started to make their favorite cookies, then I realized there was no one to eat them."

Lucy wiped her eyes and stood up. "I

think I'll go out, get some air," she said.

"You do that. I'll keep an eye on the hockey pucks."

Lucy smiled through her tears and gave Susan a hug. "Thanks."

Stepping out onto the porch, Lucy started to go down the steps to the lawn when she stopped in her tracks. All things considered, she decided that wandering off alone was not a good idea, and instead sat down on the steps. She was sitting there, lost in her thoughts, when Ben appeared, carrying a load of firewood.

"Penny for your thoughts," he said, pausing at the bottom of the steps.

"You'd be wasting your money," said Lucy, watching as he bounded up the steps with his load of logs and disappeared into the house. Moments later, he returned and sat down next to her.

"Looks like the fog is finally clearing," he said. "The ferry shouldn't have any trouble, it'll be right on schedule."

"I'm counting the minutes," confessed Lucy.

"I wish I could go," said Ben. "I have a feeling I'm going to be suspect number one when the investigation starts. I've got brown skin, I'm Latino, and I'm not from around here."

"You might as well confess and get it over with," said Lucy. She was partly joking, partly serious, and wondered how he'd react.

"That would make it easy for everyone, wouldn't it? Only problem is, I'm not guilty."

"And why should I believe you?" asked Lucy.

"Because I'm not a sociopath," said Ben. "I don't enjoy making people suffer."

"Is that what this is?"

"I think so, don't you? There doesn't seem to be any other reason."

"A vendetta against the Newman family, or against Scott?" suggested Lucy.

"Like maybe one of the Hopkins, or even all of them? A conspiracy because Scott took their island out from under them?"

"It's one theory," said Lucy.

"That means Parker's death and boys' disappearance are connected," said Ben. "They don't have to be."

"I've been thinking along those lines, too," admitted Lucy. "I wonder if Parker was pregnant and that posed a threat to the father."

"There's what, five men on the island. Anyone in particular come to mind?"

"Well, the one who would have the most

to fear in that situation would be Scott."

"Incest? Boy, you look like a nice lady, but you've got a nasty mind."

"Goes with the job," said Lucy. "Don't forget, I'm a reporter. I'm only here to write about Scott's island experiment."

"I guess you got a bigger story than you expected."

"Way bigger."

"But what about the boys? I can't imagine any father killing his sons."

"Maybe they just had a mishap and fell into the ocean. That's what Susan thinks. She says the sea took them. She's been getting messages in her dreams from the spirits."

"Well, if you're looking for someone detached from reality, there's your suspect," said Ben. He stood up and stretched. "Back to beating the bushes, but it was nice exploring the dim, dark recesses of your twisted mind."

Lucy was about to come back with a smart zinger, but she didn't have a chance before Susan popped out of the door. "Ah, Ben, I've got a job for you."

Ben grinned bashfully. "Aw, gee, I was just a minute too slow . . ."

"None of your nonsense," she said, cocking her elbow and pressing her hand against her lower back. "I want you to kill a chicken for me. I'd do it myself, but my sciatica is killing me."

"Any particular chicken, or shall I just grab the first one I see?"

Susan sighed. "I really don't care. And, Lucy, maybe you could come in and knead that bread dough for me. I've seen you in action. . . ." Her words trailed off as she limped back into the kitchen, leaving Ben and Lucy alone on the porch.

Ben narrowed his eyes and smiled at Lucy. "A woman of action, eh? And a reporter looking for a big story? Makes you wonder . . ."

Lucy's eyes widened in shock; she was the investigator, not the subject. "You can't be serious."

"Maybe you're creating the news," he said, sauntering off toward the chicken coop.

CHAPTER SEVENTEEN

The dough was sitting in a big bowl on the kitchen table, waiting for her. She washed and dried her hands, then scattered some of the flour from the canister Susan had left out for her on the table, and then peeled the sticky dough out of its bowl and plopped it into the center of the flour. She dusted her hands with flour and got started, gathering the dough together with her fingers and then pressing down with the heels of her hands. She used to do this a lot, back when she was a young mom with more time than money, and she found she was enjoying handling the elastic dough.

As she worked, her thoughts wandered to the day the boys disappeared. Oddly enough, the tongue-in-cheek A. A. Milne poem about James James Morrison's mother going to town and leaving her little son home, with its forty-shilling reward for the return of the "mislaid" mother, made her think, rather grimly, that the twins had indeed been mislaid, or lost. When she lost track of her cell phone or her car keys, she tried to remember where she'd last had them, and that usually led to her finding the lost item.

The dough had now transformed from a sticky blob to a nice, smooth ball, ready to tuck into a greased bowl covered with a clean cloth to rise. The stove was the obvious place to set it, and she waved her hand above the warm surface, looking for the perfect spot. When she found it, she set the bowl there and glanced at the clock, planning to give it an hour.

She washed her hands again, getting rid of the sticky bits that clung to her fingers, and dried them on a towel. So where had she last seen the boys? It was when she handed them each a list of things to find for the scavenger hunt, she remembered, picturing their reactions. Fred had wanted to dash off immediately, but Walter resisted. "Let's figure out a plan," he'd said, sitting down on the porch steps and studying the list. "It's a contest, stupid, the winner gets fudge," said Fred, but Walter shook his head. "It will be more fun if we do it together, and we can share the fudge." Fred had reluctantly agreed, waiting impatiently for his brother to come up with a systematic search. After a moment or two Walter announced, "Got it!" and they were off.

So, what was on the list? And how had Walter organized the search? There was sea glass, she remembered, a herring gull feather, tiny balsam pinecones . . . it was worth a try to see if she could follow in their footsteps. She remembered being struck by Walter's methodical mind when he played Monopoly, focusing on buying up property, while Fred hoarded his money and counted instead on picking a Get Out of Jail Free card.

It seemed to her that Walter probably decided to begin the search with the items that would be found in the more distant places on the island, like the beach and the forest, and would then move back toward the house. That would save energy, as they wouldn't be running hither and yon, only to retrace their steps. So once again she checked the rocky little beach where sea glass often could be found, and while she did find some nice green and blue bits of glass smoothed by the sea, she didn't find any sign of the boys.

Then she followed the dirt road that led up to the farm, through a sparse growth of balsams, noticing that there were plenty of tiny pinecones on the ground. She even found an adorable fairy house, a little shelter composed of bark and sticks, with a green moss lawn and a path outlined with pebbles tucked beneath one of the trees, and wondered who had made it. Lily, she guessed, thinking it must have been done before the boys disappeared. Perhaps intended as a surprise for them to discover. Whether they ever did or not, she didn't know.

Moving on toward the farm, she passed the Hopkinses' stone house and then paused at the icehouse, which was on the edge of the farmyard. It was locked, of course, to protect Parker's body, but she tried the door anyway, just to be sure. The door was thick and sturdy, to keep out the warm summer air and preserve the ice inside. Was it always locked, she wondered, thinking it would be quite a nuisance to unlock the door every time somebody needed ice or food. It seemed to her that the barnyard, including the icehouse, had been one of the first places that was searched when the boys were discovered to be missing, and she thought Taylor had reported there was nothing inside apart from ice and Parker's body.

Of course, no one had wanted to disturb Parker's rest, or encounter her body, so they

273

had all avoided the icehouse. Lucy thought the half-buried structure, with its low door, was a lot like those old-fashioned grass-covered tombs dug into the ground in old New England cemeteries, with their heavy iron doors. She thought of her great-grandmother's best friend, not actually a relation but called "Aunt" Etta by everyone in the family, who was terrified of being buried alive. Aunt Etta, who was a relic of the Victorian age, was not reassured by Pop-pop's insistence that such a thing was impossible because of the practice of embalming bodies. Lucy knew Aunt Etta's fears had actually been shared by many in her generation and had read of coffins with bells that could be rung in case the deceased woke up after burial.

She was thoughtful as she walked around the icehouse, hoping that Aunt Etta was resting comfortably in Susan's better place, perhaps chuckling over her foolish fears. She noticed a little clump of ghostly Indian pipes growing in a shady spot behind the icehouse and paused to admire it, noticing that one of the white stalks seemed a bit odd. Bending to take a closer look, she found a slip of paper that had been blown against the fragile stem and carefully un-furled it, discovering a fragment from one of the scavenger hunt lists.

She recognized her own handwriting and the letters *nes,* as well as *ath.* Probably pinecones and feather, she thought, smoothing out the crumpled bit of damp paper. It felt to her a bit like one of those saint's bones displayed in a fancy reliquary, a small bit of evidence proving that the boys had indeed been on this spot.

Suddenly remembering the bread dough that she'd left to rise on the stove, she checked her watch and realized she'd been gone for more than an hour. It would probably be overflowing the bowl and making a mess, she thought, hurrying back to the house.

When she got to the kitchen, she found Susan had remembered the dough and was punching it down, readying it for the second rising.

"Sorry," said Lucy, "I was out looking for the boys and I found this." She displayed the bit of paper, holding it out for Susan to see.

"Where did you find that?"

"Near the icehouse." Lucy paused. "Any chance you've got the key?"

"Taylor's got it," said Susan, replacing the clean towel over the bowl of dough. "She took it along when she and Brad checked the farmyard when the boys first went missing."

"Is there another key?" asked Lucy.

"Just the one that I know of," said Susan. "It always hung on that hook over there." Susan indicated the empty hook with a tilt of her head as she carried the bowl over to the stove. "I keep meaning to ask her to put it back, but what with everything it keeps slipping my mind."

"It's probably pointless, but I'd like to take a look in the icehouse, just to be sure," said Lucy. "I think I'll see if I can find Taylor; she's probably coming back from the puffins' nesting area by now."

Susan set the bowl down on the warm stovetop, then went over to the sink to wash her hands. "I had a dream that the boys were cold," said Susan, with a shudder. "Their little faces were blue and they had ice on their eyelashes, it was awful."

"Why didn't you say something?" asked Lucy.

"Nobody takes my ramblings seriously," said Susan. "Everybody thinks I'm just making it up, trying to get attention."

Lucy had to admit she was among the guilty; she had joked with Ben about Susan's contacts with the spirit world just this morning. But now she felt rather ashamed.

"We definitely need to look in that ice-house," said Lucy, "and I'm sorry if you thought I wasn't taking you seriously."

"No matter," said Susan, drying her hands with a towel. "Even I have my doubts and wonder if I've got an overactive imagination. That's what my mother called it."

"That's not a bad thing. You're probably very sensitive to signs the rest of us are too dense to notice. I think they call it EQ, emotional quotient. It's kind of like IQ, but it means you're able to sense shifts in people's feelings." She grabbed the door-knob. "I'll be back with the key."

As she strode across the lawn, happy to have a reason for action, she thought about Susan, wondering if she really was able to see things that most people couldn't see. There was a lot of research now about tells, the subtle signs that indicated a person was lying, or bluffing. A slight tic in an eye, for example, or a tapping foot. There were experts who claimed they could accurately determine if a person was truthful or not, and some of them had written books sharing their insights.

Lucy had been mildly interested, but didn't quite believe them. She thought it was probably a hoax, like mesmerism, or phrenology. But now she wondered if there

277

was something to it, and maybe Susan did have an uncanny ability to sense subtleties other people missed. Maybe she'd been worried that Taylor didn't search the icehouse thoroughly, or maybe Brad had said something that set off alarm bells in Susan's head that later appeared to her as a vision of the twins' blue faces.

It was really too dreadful to think that the boys might have been locked in the icehouse all this time, in the cold, with their sister's dead body. She hoped it wasn't the case, but she had to find out. It was her father who had always urged her to double- and triple-check everything. Look over that check before you mail it to make sure the figures are correct; read that letter after you write it, wait a bit, and read it again before you send it; and call the store before you go to make sure they have the item you want in stock, and while you're at it, ask when they're open. It was in that spirit that she wanted to revisit the icehouse, just to make sure the boys hadn't gotten themselves trapped in there.

She knew boys had a knack for getting themselves in trouble, and she thought the twins might very well have wanted to take a good look at a dead body. People often assumed that children couldn't understand death, or would find it traumatic, but Lucy's experience did not support that notion. Toby, and the girls, too, had been fascinated by the hunting trophies left around the yard by the family cat. They would gather around the sad remains of a mouse or a vole to study it and would then hurry into the house to announce what they'd found.

A sister, even a half sister, was a different proposition, and you might think the boys would be upset by her death, but Lucy hadn't noticed any special closeness between Parker and the twins. On the contrary, it seemed both Parker and Taylor had considered the boys to be major nuisances and had repeatedly warned them off. Lucy had seen a similar dynamic play out in her house, when Sara and Zoe had felt that Patrick was an impediment to their plans, especially when those plans involved a boyfriend. It wouldn't surprise Lucy at all if the twins had somehow managed to get themselves locked in the icehouse while everyone was out searching for them on the rest of the island.

She'd been striding along on automatic, following the well-trodden path through the woods while her mind wandered off on paths of its own, when she noticed a large feather lying on the ground. She stooped to pick it up, admiring the rich brown color and the finely detailed construction that allowed the vanes of the feather to zip and unzip. Birds were such amazing creatures, she thought, thinking of those cute little puffins spending most of their lives alone, out on the sea, bobbing on the waves. A person sure couldn't do that, but a puffin had all sorts of adaptations that allowed it to survive cold and wet, even storms, and then enabled it to fly hundreds of miles back to the breeding area, and even to the very nesting burrow where it was hatched, to mate and raise another generation.

As she walked, she swished the feather back and forth, noticing how it produced resistance in the air that allowed the bird to fly. She could feel the lift in her hand, it felt as if the feather itself wanted to take off and fly. What would it be like, she wondered, to be able to stretch out your wings and fly? To soar high into the sky and look down at Earth below? What did trees look like from up there, and fields, and the sea? She knew that avian vision was different from human sight, and that birds could spot tiny movements that signaled prey from great distances. It was that ability that allowed them to spot an unsuspecting mouse or rabbit going about its business, and to swoop down and snatch it up in their talons. She'd seen it happen in her own backyard, and it was all over so quickly that she could hardly believe what she'd seen.

That's when she heard the shriek, the sound that a redtail makes, and paused to look skyward in hopes of seeing the creature circling high above her. Instead, what she saw was the feathered breast of the bird only a few feet above her, with its talons ready to strike. She instinctively raised her arm and the bird raked her skin, leaving it striped and bloody. Surprised and caught off guard, she stood for a moment, looking at her wounded arm and trying to figure out what had happened, when the bird struck again, this time scraping her shoulder with its talons and giving her head a powerful whack with its wing that sent her reeling. The blow was so forceful that it knocked her off her feet, sending her to the ground, where she hit her head on a rock. The last thing she heard before everything went black was that screech, the wild cry of the redtail.

Lucy came to a few minutes later, hardly able to believe what had happened. She was lying on her back and the trees above her were blurry, but as her vision cleared she noticed a large nest constructed of sticks. That explained it, she thought, she'd come too close to the redtail's nest.

"Well, how was I to know?" she demanded, yelling at the bird. Her right arm was a bloody mess, and stung like hell, and she knew those wounds needed to be cleaned as soon as possible because Lord knows where those talons had been before they ripped into her arm. Her head was pounding, and when she gingerly patted it with her good arm she found a large goose egg behind her left ear. She sat for a moment, then decided she'd better get moving before the hawk decided to attack again. Without thinking, she instinctively made the usual move to rise from the ground, only to realize her right arm would not cooperate. She couldn't move it to lever herself up from the ground and, gently probing it with her left hand, discovered that her right shoulder was also injured. She didn't know how deep the bird's talons had penetrated, but they had definitely done some damage.

She laid back on the ground, keeping a wary eye out for the bird, and considered her options. She couldn't care for her wounds — she hadn't thought to bring a first-aid kit for her walk through the woods — and she was only dressed in shorts and a T shirt. She didn't even have a bandana to tie around her arm, or to use as a sling for her injured arm. What to do? The adrenaline that had surged through her body was abating, leaving her feeling very shaky. She knew she couldn't go far; she doubted she could make it all the way back to the house. Her only alternative was to continue on toward the puffin nesting area, hopefully meeting Taylor as she returned from her morning's work there. Taylor always carried a first-aid kit, along with the rest of the equipment she needed for the puffin study, and could help her.

Moving very carefully, cradling her injured arm against her chest, Lucy sat up. She was a little woozy, so she waited a few minutes until she felt better; then she folded her legs and used her left arm to push herself up onto her knees. Everything whirled around her for a moment or two, so she concentrated on some slow, deep breathing. When the earth stopped spinning, she got her left foot on the ground, then the right, and still cradling her injured arm with the other, got to her feet.

This is going to be painful, she told herself, and she was right. Every step, every little movement hurt her arm and shoulder, but she had no choice but to go on. Right foot, left foot, breathe, she told herself, over and over. She recognized a twisted balsam and realized she didn't have far to go; the nesting ground was just a little way beyond it. Right foot, left foot, breathe. Almost there.

And then she saw Taylor, sitting at the far end of the nesting ground, making a notation on a clipboard. She slipped her pen beneath the clip and stood up, and that's when she noticed Lucy. Her eyes widened and her mouth fell open in shock. "My gosh, what happened to you?"

CHAPTER EIGHTEEN

"A hawk," said Lucy. "That redtail attacked me."

"The one with the nest near the trail?" asked Taylor, making her way cautiously through the treacherous nesting area. She was wearing short rubber boots and a fisherman's vest with lots of pockets over her jeans and T-shirt, and had a pack on her back.

"The very same. I guess she thought I got a bit too close."

"I've heard that they will do that," said Taylor, dropping her pack on the ground. "I know there's a first-aid kit in here somewhere," she said, digging through the contents and finally finding it at the very bottom, where it had settled. "Ah, here it is."

Lucy perched on a boulder, cradling her arm.

"I haven't checked it lately. I hope it's all here," said Taylor, opening the white plastic box with the red cross on the lid and examining the contents. "It's clearly not designed for anything as major as your injuries," she commented, producing a small packet containing a tidy wipe and ripping it open.

She unfolded the wipe and dabbed carefully at Lucy's injuries, cleaning up some of the blood. The stripes of torn skin had mostly stopped bleeding and were beginning to scab over, so they decided not to attempt to bandage them with the assorted Band-Aids provided in the kit, which were too small in any case. "Your wounds need to be cleaned properly, but we can't do it here. Susan's a good nurse, you know. She even delivered a few babies when there were more people on the island."

Lucy wasn't terribly reassured. She had a brutal headache, her arm throbbed with pain, and in addition to a serious painkiller, she knew she needed a tetanus shot and an antibiotic, neither of which was available on the island. Trying not to think of gangrene or some horrible flesh-eating bacteria, she watched as Taylor unfolded the square of white cloth that was included in the kit, shook it out, and refolded it into a triangle. Once the cloth was arranged beneath Lucy's arm, Taylor stood behind her and reached over her shoulders for the ends of the cloth so she could tie them behind Lucy's neck to make a sling.

At that moment, when she knew she should feel nothing but gratitude for Taylor's care, she instead felt the hairs on the back of her neck rise. What did she fear? Did she really think Taylor was going to strangle her with the cloth? She brushed away the thought, wondering if this was like one of Susan's insightful moments. If so, she decided, it wasn't ESP or EQ or anything like that at all. It was simply a reflexive response by her nervous system when Taylor's fingers brushed the back of her neck. That was all, period.

"Your head's bloody, too," said Taylor, finishing the knot and gently probing the area with her hand. "You've got quite a goose egg."

Reflexively, Lucy brushed away Taylor's hand. "That hurt."

"Sorry," said Taylor. "There's aspirin in the first-aid kit. Do you want some?"

"Better not," said Lucy, opting for caution. "It might make me bleed more."

"Right," said Taylor. "How come you came out here, anyway?"

Once again, Lucy felt that frisson of fear. "Oh, I almost forgot. I came to get the key to the icehouse. Susan said you had it."

"Why do you want it?" asked Taylor, her voice studiedly casual.

She was still standing behind Lucy, resting one hand on Lucy's good shoulder.

"Uh, Susan wants it," said Lucy, not quite ready to show her hand. "I said I'd come and get it for her."

"Why does Susan want it? I thought she cleared all the food out."

The hand on her shoulder felt heavier, so Lucy leaned forward and stood up, facing Taylor. She didn't want to feel like a sitting duck; she wanted to see Taylor's face and gauge her reactions. "She had a dream that the boys were in there." Lucy rolled her eyes. "You know how she is, always getting messages from beyond."

"Well, the boys are definitely not in there. I looked very carefully." She sniffed and pressed her lips together. "It was hard, I didn't want to go in, because of Parker being there. Her body, you know?" She gazed off into the distance, blinking furiously. "She was my sister, my twin. We were really close."

Lucy's memory was somewhat different; she remembered Taylor volunteering to check the barnyard, including the icehouse. In fact, thought Lucy, she had actually claimed to have a twisted ankle that made it too difficult for her to explore the north side of the island, which Scott had asked her to do. The ankle injury must have been very slight, thought Lucy, recalling that it hadn't seemed to bother Taylor in recent days. Out here near the cliff edge certainly wasn't the place to confront Taylor, however, so she offered sympathy instead. "That must have been very difficult for you," she said. "I think Susan might be thinking that the boys could have sneaked in while everyone was out looking for them. I have a son and a grandson, so I know how naughty boys can be."

"Surely not Walter and Fred," replied Taylor, failing to sound as sincere as she had intended. "They're little angels."

Lucy desperately hoped that was not the case, and that the boys had not yet reached Susan's better place but were here on earth, alive and waiting to be found.

"And besides, there's only the one key, and I have it."

"Maybe the boys found another key somewhere. Keys have a way of getting forgotten, left on hooks, or in drawers. And little boys are full of mischief and love to poke into things. Didn't they snoop on you quite a bit?"

It was then that Lucy realized she had struck a nerve, when Taylor's eyes widened and she set her jaw. What if the boys had seen something, maybe something connected with Parker's death, and that's why they disappeared? Aware that she had stumbled into dangerous territory, Lucy hastened to contain the damage. "Not that they would have seen you doing anything except sunbathe, that sort of thing . . ."

"They did love to spy on me and Parker," said Taylor.

Lucy nodded and smiled. She really wanted to get away from Taylor. "Well, thanks for your help," she said. "I guess there's nothing for it but to start back to the house." Pretty much every muscle in her body hurt, and she couldn't go very fast, but she sensed that continuing this discussion with Taylor was dangerous. She wasn't ready to believe that Taylor had killed her sister and the boys, but the thought had reared its ugly head and she knew it would hang around her consciousness until it was proven false — which she most earnestly hoped it would be. In the meantime, she thought she would rather be safe than sorry.

"I'll go with you," said Taylor, picking up her pack and swinging it onto her back. "I was just about finished here, anyway."

"Great," said Lucy, wishing she felt as enthusiastic as she sounded. She was inwardly calculating her chances of making it back to the house alive and decided she certainly wanted to keep Taylor in view while they walked. "You go ahead," she said. "I don't want to slow you down."

"Oh, no. I'd better follow, in case you stumble or fall."

Lucy definitely did not want to go into the woods ahead of Taylor. The woods were full of possible weapons like rocks and sticks that Taylor could use to hit her on the head. It would be easy enough to explain the fatal injury as an accident, especially since she already had a head wound that could very well have made her woozy and unsteady on her feet. But what were her options? To insist on going behind, alerting Taylor to her suspicions? Or to plead weakness and stay in the nesting area, presumably waiting for Taylor to send rescuers? That seemed like a pretty good idea, she decided, figuring that sooner or later she'd be missed.

"I don't think I can make it," Lucy said, putting her hand to her head. "It would be best if you went ahead and sent help."

"You're just going to sit here and wait?"

"Yeah, you go ahead. I'll probably feel stronger in a bit."

"But it's getting cooler," said Taylor. "You might get chilled, or you might pass out from that bump on the head."

Lucy was beginning to doubt herself and her reactions. Maybe Taylor really did have her best interests at heart. Or maybe she wanted to kill her in the woods. She really didn't know what to think. Her body, however, was definitely in favor of a little rest. "I'll be okay," she said.

"Well, if you insist on staying, there's a nice little spot, quite sheltered, just over there," said Taylor, with a wave of her hand. "I'll show you. Follow me."

Lucy hesitated, looking around rather hopefully. The breeze had picked up and she was rather chilly in her T-shirt; getting behind some sort of windbreak seemed a good idea. But where was it? There was no obvious sheltered spot in the nesting area.

"C'mon," urged Taylor. "It's just over here."

Lucy yawned. She was really very tired, and it couldn't hurt to take a look, could it? So she followed Taylor as she weaved her way between the puffins' nesting burrows back toward the cliff edge. "Not too close," she muttered, as she stumbled along, noticing that her field of vision seemed to be narrowing. She stopped, realizing that this growing blackness that was closing in on her vision meant she was losing consciousness. Quickly, she plopped herself down, sticking her head between her legs.

She was sitting there for some minutes before Taylor realized Lucy was no longer following her. Lucy heard her exclaim, "What?" and then heard her crunching back through the scrubby brush that covered the nesting area. "Are you okay?" she asked.

"Mmm," said Lucy, lifting her head and discovering the blackness was receding. "Just resting," she said thickly, her chin falling back onto her chest.

"Well, come along. You can rest better over here." Taylor took Lucy's good arm and pulled her to her feet, then wrapping her arm around Lucy's waist, she led her on toward the cliff edge.

"Uh, no, no," protested Lucy. The blackness was coming back, and she was so tired. She didn't want to move.

"Just a few steps more," urged Taylor, dragging her along.

Lucy couldn't see much, but she sensed the coolness of the air and heard the surf crashing on the rocks below. She pulled away from Taylor, landing on her bottom. Good, she thought, solid ground. She intended to stay there.

Taylor had other ideas and tried to pull Lucy to her feet, even grabbing her injured arm, which made Lucy yelp with pain. She instinctively kicked out at Taylor, who released her, but only briefly. Lucy felt Taylor's hands reaching under her arms, attempting to pull her to her feet. Crazily, she laughed, thinking to herself: *Good thing I waited to start Weight Watchers — I've still got those ten extra pounds.*

Taylor was huffing and puffing with the effort. Lucy could hear her panting and, opening her eyes, saw her face right in front of hers, red from exertion. *Not a good look for her,* she thought, flopping onto her back. Looking up, she saw the clearing sky filled with puffins, returning to their burrows carrying fish in their colorful beaks for their nestlings. "Wow," she said, amazed at the sight.

"Come on!" yelled Taylor. "Get up!"

"Nnnooo," said Lucy, shaking her head and immediately realizing that was a bad idea. Pain shot behind her eyes, and the darkness was coming back. She could feel Taylor grabbing her ankles and pulling her along. She tried to resist by grabbing at the scrubby bushes, but she had only the one good arm. *What a way to end,* she thought, *rolled over a cliff into the ocean. Would they ever find her? Would Bill and the kids miss her?* She scrabbled around frantically, reaching for anything, and found a burrow opening. She shoved her arm in as far as it would go and with every bit of strength she possessed, she pressed against the earth wall of the burrow, stopping her body's progress toward the cliff edge.

In the sky above her, a returning puffin intent on feeding its nestling flapped furiously, protesting the intrusion into its burrow. It opened its beak to squawk and dropped a mouthful of fish. Lucy saw the silvery little fish flipping and flopping in slow motion as they fell to the ground behind Taylor. Taylor, still intent on rolling her over the cliff, didn't notice and stepped right on the slippery fish. Her feet flew out from under her and she landed flat on her back, inches from the edge.

Fearing Taylor was down, but not out, Lucy struggled to withdraw her arm from the burrow, hampered by the frantic puffins, which hovered above her, dive-bombing and flapping their wings around her face. The little nestling in the burrow was also participating in the attack, having heard its parents, and was snapping at her hand with its little beak. She was wiggling away on her back, trying to get her arm out, when Taylor reappeared, looming above her and batting away the puffins.

Don't give up, she told herself, but the blackness was coming back and she was so tired. *What was the point? She was alone out here, injured, unable to defend herself, with a physically fit psychopath. There was no way . . .*

It was then that she heard a strong, masculine voice yell, "Hey! What's going on?" She turned her head toward the sound and made out two shadowy figures hurrying across the nesting area toward her. And then they were there, beside her, gently raising her head and giving her sips of water.

"She tried to push me over the edge," claimed Taylor. "Thank goodness you came."

Brad gave her a doubtful look. "Well, if that's really true, it looks like you managed to defend yourself pretty well. Lucy here looks to be in pretty bad shape."

"The redtail got me," whispered Lucy. "And then Taylor dragged me over here. . . ."

"I was only trying to help her to a sheltered spot while I went for help," insisted Taylor.

"Is that true?" asked Will, helping Lucy to sit up.

"I don't know, I really don't know," said Lucy, whose mind was a jumble.

"Mom said you came out here to get the icehouse key from Taylor," said Will.

"Yeah. Do you have it?" asked Brad.

"Taylor's got it," said Lucy.

"Is this what you want?" asked Taylor, reaching into one of the vest pockets and pulling out the large, old-fashioned key and dangling it, teasingly, in front of Will. A sly look came over her face and she impetuously threw it over the cliff edge and into the sea.

"Dumb move, Taylor," said Will. "We can break down the door."

"Well, you won't find anything except my dear departed sister's rotting body," said Taylor, with a shrug.

"We'll see," said Brad. "But first we've got to get Lucy back to the house. Do you think you can walk, with help?" he asked.

"I think so," said Lucy. "If you help me get my arm out of this hole."

They made an odd little procession as they made their way back along the path through the tall fir trees. Lucy tried to walk, but her progress was so slow that Will and Brad scooped her up and carried her between them, cradled in their arms. Taylor dragged along behind them, kicking at the ground like a resentful toddler, muttering to herself.

When they broke out of the woods, by the farm, Hopp and Susan ran to help them. "Get an ax," yelled Brad. "We have to break down the icehouse door."

"What?" It was Scott confronting them. "What door are you breaking down?"

"The icehouse. The boys . . ." said Lucy, as Will and Brad carefully set her down on a rock wall. Susan was immediately at her side, supporting her and clucking over her wounds.

"The boys are in the icehouse?" It was Lily, a grieving madonna right out of a Renaissance painting in a blue shawl, who had come from the vegetable garden clutching a bunch of scallions instead of lilies.

"Maybe," said Brad. "We have to check."

"Where is the key?" asked Scott.

"Taylor threw it away," said Will.

"Is that true?" asked Lily, turning to Taylor.

"Maybe," replied Taylor, with a shrug.

"We have to find out if the boys are in there," said Lily, pleading with her husband. "Break open the door."

Hopp had already returned from the wood shed with a large ax, which he gave to Brad. By now Ben and Wolf had also joined the group, wondering what was going on, and they marched across the farmyard to the icehouse with Brad. Will remained with the women, keeping a watchful eye on Taylor.

Lucy had a clear view of the icehouse, and she heard the crack of the wood as Brad heaved the ax into the door. It took several more whacks before the door split and the men were able to pull it apart. Hopp went in and moments later emerged with Fred, limp in his arms. Ben immediately dove in after him and brought out Walter, who was wrapped in a sheet, the same sheet they had used to cover Parker's body.

"My boys," sighed Lily, collapsing in a dead faint.

CHAPTER NINETEEN

Susan was indeed an expert nurse, initiating triage right there in the farmyard. She first checked each of the boys, determining they were breathing, albeit shallowly, and were still hanging on to life but suffering from hypothermia. She ordered Brad and Hopp to carry them into her house, where they should close the windows and build a fire, strip off their chilly, damp clothing, and wrap them in blankets. Ben and Wolf immediately went to help them; Ben held the door open for the two men carrying the boys, and Wolf gathered up an armful of firewood from the stack by the door.

Then she turned her attention briefly to Lily, ordering Scott to rouse her and take her inside to the boys, where they should strip off their clothes and press their warm bodies against the boys' cold ones. "Wrap yourselves up with them in the blankets, and whatever you do, don't rub their arms or feet — that could kill them. Concentrate on warming their trunks, but be very gentle."

Scott nodded and bent over his wife, who was beginning to stir, and helped her to her feet. "The boys!" she exclaimed as she stood up. "Are they . . . ?"

"They're alive, baby, alive," said Scott, embracing his wife. "We have to warm them up. They're in the farmhouse."

He had no sooner spoken than Lily was running, angelic in her fluttering blue robes and streaming blond hair, hastening to tend to her boys. Scott ran with her, holding her hand as they took the porch steps two at a time.

Lucy had been caught up in the dramatic discovery of the boys in the icehouse, followed by Scott and Lily's touching scene, and was still sitting on the wall, exhausted, when Susan approached her. It was then, as Susan gently unwrapped the sling and studied her injuries, that she remembered her struggle with Taylor in the nesting area high above the roiling sea below. "Taylor tried to kill me," she said, peeking warily over Susan's shoulder in an effort to locate her attacker. "She put the boys in the icehouse, and I think she killed Parker."

"Now why would she do all that?" asked

Susan in a doubtful tone. "There must be some other explanation."

"She even threw the icehouse key into the ocean," said Lucy, bolstering her argument. She had spotted Taylor, some distance away on the lawn, wrestling with Brad, who was trying to restrain her.

"Look!" said Lucy, and Susan turned to see Taylor struggling with Brad. She was wriggling and kicking, scratching at his face, and finally managed to knee his groin. He fell to the ground, clutching himself and moaning, and she headed for the woods, where she vanished among the trees.

Susan left Lucy and rushed over to her son, who was writhing on the ground. "Ice would be the best thing . . ." she said, just as Hopp came out of the house.

"What happened?" he demanded, rushing to his grandson's side.

"Taylor kicked him in his privates," said Susan. "Do you think you could get some ice?"

He nodded and ran toward the icehouse, disappearing inside and emerging a few minutes later with a good-size chunk. Seeing this, Susan unzipped her son's jeans and ordered him to apply the ice. Leaving Hopp in charge, she returned to Lucy.

"Hopp! How are the boys?" asked Lucy,

raising her voice as loud as she could, which wasn't actually very loud.

"Hopp! The boys?" yelled Susan. "How are they doing?"

"Walter's opened his eyes, he's mumbling. Fred's breathing easier. They're warming up good."

"I'll be with them in a minute. First I want to grab some herbs for Lucy's wounds."

While Susan hurried off to the garden, Lucy sat, holding her injured arm, trying to sort out everything that had happened. She now believed that Taylor had killed her sister, locked the twins in the icehouse, and tried to kill her, but like Susan, she couldn't imagine why. Why would a beautiful young woman, rich and talented, with the whole world at her feet, do such terrible things? The only explanation she could come up with was that Taylor was mentally ill, perhaps even psychotic. But that didn't really seem satisfactory. And where was she now? What was she doing? Was she planning some other terrible deed, like burning down the house? Or maybe killing herself? What was going to happen to her? They needed to find her and restrain her, if only to protect her from herself.

That's what she told Susan, when she returned with a huge bunch of basil. Susan wasn't convinced. "First things first," she said. "Let's get you fixed up." She helped Lucy get to her feet and up the steps, through the back door into the kitchen. There she sat Lucy at the kitchen table and started running water and gathering cloths.

"I can see the wounds on your arm," she said, speaking slowly and directly to Lucy. "What hurts that I can't see?"

"My head," said Lucy, pointing behind her ear, "and my shoulder."

Susan gently felt the lump on Lucy's head and pronounced it "Not too bad." Then she gently unbuttoned her shirt, revealing the wound on her shoulder. "Hawk, I'd guess."

Lucy nodded.

Susan clucked a bit, washing the puncture wounds on Lucy's shoulder. "Your tetanus shot up to date?" she asked.

"I haven't got a clue," said Lucy.

"Well, no matter. We just have to get you on the ferry tomorrow and back to the ER in Tinker's Cove. They can take proper care of you. Meanwhile, I'm going to make a compress with the basil, it fights infection." She sighed. "It's the best I can do."

"I'll smell good," said Lucy, her head falling onto her chest.

"And I think you'd better have some tea with sugar," said Susan, putting on the kettle. "I suspect you've got a concussion, so I don't think you should sleep."

Fortified with sugary tea and reeking of basil, Lucy took a peek into the Hopkinses' small living room. There she saw Walter sitting up, wrapped in a thick Hudson's Bay blanket, sipping hot cocoa from a cup held by his father. Fred was still cocooned in a blanket with his mother, lying face-to-face on their sides in front of the blazing fire. Ben and Wolf were taking turns tending the fire, and she stopped Wolf when he stepped out into the hall on his way to get more firewood.

"Taylor's out there," she said. "We've got to find her."

"She can't go far on this island," said Wolf, with a shrug.

"She's dangerous, to herself and to us, too."

"I'll keep an eye out," he said, reaching for the doorknob.

She watched as he stepped outside, then followed, to see how Brad was doing. He was no longer lying on the lawn, so she assumed he was feeling better. She was suddenly concerned for them, with Taylor on the loose, when she heard voices from the kitchen. She found Brad and Hopp there, where Susan was advising more ice and rest.

"We have to secure the icehouse," said Hopp. "Don't want animals getting to poor Parker's body, now do we?"

"I don't want you out there alone," said Susan. "Get Ben or Wolf to help you."

"I can help," said Brad, who was sitting white-faced on a chair, holding the ice against his groin.

"You need to sit a while and take it easy. I don't need anybody's help to nail up a few boards, and I'm not afraid of that girl," said Hopp, heading for the door.

"Don't underestimate her. Look what she did to Brad," said Susan, with a nod in his direction. Brad was clearly still in considerable pain, clenching his jaw and taking regular yoga breaths.

"Point taken," said Hopp, changing direction and going to find a helper. He'd only been gone a few minutes when Scott came into the kitchen, asking for soup for the boys.

"How are they doing?" asked Susan, getting out a pot.

"They're both hungry," said Scott. "Fred's awake now; he had a tougher time, I think, because he's thinner and less well-insulated than Walter." Suddenly overcome with emotion and exhaustion, he plopped down on a chair at the kitchen table, shaking his head.

"Walter says Taylor tricked them into going into the icehouse, said they should see if Parker was still there or if she'd gone to heaven, like Jesus."

"Oh, my Lord." Susan fumbled and dropped the can opener she was using to open the soup, then picked it up and started over. "Why would she do such an evil thing? Lock them up and leave them to die?"

"I don't know," said Scott, shaking his head. "She's always been impulsive and quick to lash out, even as a little girl. I knew I was taking a risk when I named Parker as a partner in the firm. I knew it would upset Taylor, she's like that, very competitive. Jealous, even. I thought she'd be content with the PR job, but I was wrong. I think she must have been furious with me, and with Parker. I think she locked up the boys to get back at me, and Lily, of course. She never got on well with Lily." He shook his head. "I underestimated her. I didn't realize how upset she was, and the lengths she'd go to."

Listening to him, Lucy remembered encountering him in the woods that night, heavily armed and patrolling against imagined invaders, and thought the apple didn't fall far from the tree. As far as she was concerned, Scott's insistence on returning the island to the nineteenth century and his decision to acquire a private arsenal for protection indicated he was mentally unstable to the point of being dangerous. His decision to shun modern advances had put his own family and the other islanders at risk. Taylor, who perhaps had inherited her father's mental instability, had merely gone one step further.

"Here's the soup," said Susan, handing him a tray with two bowls. "Just broth, and not too hot, either. They should take it slowly."

Scott stood up and took the tray. "Thanks for taking such good care of us," he told Susan, thick-voiced with emotion and blinking furiously. "I haven't been very good to you."

"I've got no complaints," said Susan in a no-nonsense voice. "Now go take care of those boys."

After he'd gone, and she was alone with Susan, Lucy spoke up. "We have to find Taylor. She's a real threat. What if she knows about Scott's weapons?"

"Weapons? What do you mean?"

"I saw him out the other night patrolling the perimeters, that's what he called it. He had an assault rifle and I don't know what all. He said he had plenty of armaments to defend the island from invaders."

Susan's face clouded over. "Do you know where this cache is?"

"No," said Lucy, "but I bet Taylor does."

"Good Lord," sighed Susan, as Hopp returned.

"The icehouse is all secure," he said, sounding satisfied. "Ferry's due tomorrow and we'll get everything sorted out."

"If Taylor doesn't blow us all to kingdom come," said Susan.

"What do you mean?" demanded Hopp.

"Lucy here says Scott has an arms cache, in case the island is invaded."

"That's crazy," said Hopp, dismissively.

"Yeah," said Lucy. "It is crazy, but I saw him, armed to the teeth with his face blacked out, dressed in camouflage. At the very least we've got to find out if he really does have these weapons and where he keeps them. Then we can guard them and make sure Taylor doesn't get them."

Hopp was silent, thinking things over. Finally, he came to a decision. "Okay. We'll go together and talk to him."

When they entered the living room they saw that both boys were sitting up, still wrapped in blankets, and were being spoon-fed warming broth by their parents.

"They were very brave," said Lily, beaming with pride and relief. "They clung together for warmth and used the straw from the ice as insulation, wrapping themselves in the sheet that was over Parker's body. They took turns yelling for help."

"I knew we could survive," said Fred. "I read a book about Shackleton's expedition."

"He walked across Antarctica, after his ship was icebound," added Walter. "He saved almost everyone in his crew."

"They stayed calm, they didn't panic," said Scott. "And you boys didn't panic, either. I'm really proud of you."

"The boys were very brave," said Lucy, "but we need to talk to you for a minute. It's important."

"What now?" cried Lily in a shrill voice.

"Nothing, babe. I'll take care of it," said Scott. He set the bowl of soup on the coffee table and went out into the hall, along with Lucy and Hopp. The three formed a tight little circle.

"It's about the weapons you're storing here on the island," began Lucy.

"We're worried that Taylor might get her hands on them," added Hopp.

Scott's eyes widened and he sank onto the hall chair, slapping his forehead with his hand. "I've been so stupid."

"She knows about them?" asked Lucy.

"Not only knows about them . . . I trained her to use them."

"Let's go," said Hopp. "Where are they?"

Scott got to his feet and walked heavily out the kitchen door and across the farmyard to the huge barn, where he led the way down the stairs in one of the silos to the cellar. Lucy and Hopp followed, clattering down the wooden steps, into the cool dark of the stone-lined basement. Lucy had been expecting Scott to light one of the oil lanterns that were the usual source of light on the island, but much to her surprise, he flicked a switch and generator-powered industrial lights illuminated the whole space. Environmentalism only went so far, she thought cynically, following him as he led the way to a thick wooden door that was secured with a heavy metal hasp and a combination padlock. The padlock, however, was looped into the hasp, hanging open.

"I'm afraid we're too late," said Scott, unhooking the open padlock and pulling the door open.

Lucy gasped with shock; she'd never seen so many weapons. Not just guns but cases of grenades and ammunition, even rocket launchers. It was like something out of a movie, when the evil arms dealers reveal the weapons they are offering to sell to the terrorists. Those scenes often ended in a shoot-out, she thought, nervously glancing around.

"What's missing?" asked Hopp, all business.

"A couple of assault rifles, a couple of handguns, ammo, and . . ." Scott was bent over a wooden crate that had been opened. "Mines."

"Land mines?" asked Lucy, incredulous. Who stocked their cellar with mines?

"No, underwater."

"The ferry," said Hopp.

"What are we going to do?" demanded Lucy, both terrified and furious. The ferry was her way out of this situation and now Taylor was planning to blow it up? Hell no.

"Don't worry," said Hopp, displaying the same calm, cool, and calculating demeanor that Shackleton was famous for. "I have a plan."

"I sure hope so," said Scott. His voice was the voice of a man who couldn't take much more. A man who'd seen his dreams, his illusions, even his fantasies shattered. A man who'd brought death and destruction to his family.

CHAPTER TWENTY

The next morning, after a tense and busy night when everyone had crowded together in the farmhouse for safety, and only the twin boys got any sleep, Hopp's plan was finally set in motion. The long week of fog had finally broken and the dawn brought a bright, sunny day, along with a brisk breeze. It was such a perfect day, and everything on the island looked so clean and beautiful that Lucy almost wished she could stay. It was only a fleeting thought, with a big *if only things were different*. The fly in the ointment was Taylor, who had not been seen all night, but was most certainly lurking nearby, armed and dangerous.

Instead of waiting on the dock, along with her bags, Lucy was standing on the farmhouse porch, crouching behind a rose of Sharon bush and peering through binoculars, waiting for the ferry to approach one of the buoys that marked the safe channel to the island. When that happened, she was going to signal Scott, who had taken up a sheltered position with a clear view of the dock, and he was going to shoot the mines that Taylor had planted, detonating a huge explosion that would be clearly visible from the ferry but would not harm it.

Her heart was racing as she watched the ferry make its steady progress toward the island, and she could only imagine what was going through Scott's mind. She thought also of the island men, who had crept out before dawn and were armed and positioned strategically with orders to capture or, if necessary, kill Taylor. And where, she wondered, was Taylor hidden, waiting to witness her planned ferry explosion?

Now, now was the moment, realized Lucy, as the ferry reached the buoy. She lifted the whistle Scott had given her to her lips and blew for all she was worth. A staccato of shots rang out, and the mines detonated in a deafening explosion, tossing shredded planks into the air along with a huge, billowing column of black smoke. Flames shot upward, and in a matter of moments the pier was completely destroyed.

Lucy watched through the binoculars as the ferry rode out the ensuing large wave produced by the explosion, and she prayed the captain was reporting the explosion and calling for help, as Hopp had predicted he would. How long would it take for the Coast Guard to arrive? And how would Taylor react to the premature detonation?

At the moment, it was spookily quiet, with no sign of any living thing on the island except for the red-tailed hawk, who had apparently been disturbed by the explosion and was circling high in the sky above, keeping a watchful eye on the island below. Lucy decided it would be prudent to abandon her exposed position on the porch and went inside the house, careful to lock the door behind her.

Inside, Susan and Lily, as well as Hopp, were gathered with the boys in the hall, near the cellar stairs. If there was any hostile activity outside, any sign of Taylor, they were ready to retreat to the safety of the basement. But for now, there was nothing. It was like waiting for a hurricane to approach, or a tornado.

Then they were startled by a whirring noise, an approaching helicopter. Lucy ran into the kitchen and pushed aside the checked curtain that covered the window, amazed to see a white helicopter with a red stripe slowly descending to land in the farmyard. The Coast Guard had arrived.

As she watched, Scott appeared from his vantage point in the bushes next to the icehouse and ran toward the helicopter, ducking down to avoid the whirring blades. As soon as he appeared there was a short burst of fire from above. Lucy realized that Taylor had positioned herself in the top of the silo that rose from the side of the barn! Scott clutched his shoulder, at least one of the bullets must have hit him, but kept on running to the copter. Armed officers were already coming out of the copter and sheltering behind it.

"Down, we have to go down," hissed Lily, and Lucy realized they weren't safe even in the house. Taylor's high-powered rifle, combined with her advantageous position, gave her complete control of the situation. They were all targets, and she didn't doubt that Taylor would shoot to kill.

Together, they hurried down and huddled at the bottom of the cellar stairs, alert for any sound from above. "I hope she doesn't blow us all to kingdom come," whispered Susan, and Lucy prayed harder than she had ever prayed for peace.

She wasn't alone. She heard Lily, in the faintest voice possible, repeating over and over, "It's going to be okay, it's going to be okay."

The boys, bundled in matching hoodies and sweatpants, had rolled themselves into balls, sitting with their arms wrapped around their ankles.

Then the silence was broken by Scott's voice, amplified on a megaphone. "Taylor, it's over. The state police are coming, a Coast Guard cutter is coming, give yourself up. We love you, we'll support you, you'll be safe."

The only answer was the staccato sound of her gun, firing, and then a sudden explosion.

Lucy was halfway up the stairs before she thought that she might be rushing into danger, but she pushed the thought aside. She had to know what was going on. Reaching the top of the stairs, she pushed the door open and crawled out onto her hands and knees, immediately aware of the smell of burning oil and metal. Returning to the kitchen window, she peeked out and saw flames spurting from the helicopter's rotor motor, its twisted rotors still slowly spinning. Two of the crewmembers were dragging Scott away from the burning wreckage, two others were lying motionless on the ground.

She crawled over to the kitchen door and opened it, then ducked back as more shots rang out. Just then the wind picked up, creating a cloud of oily black smoke that screened the fleeing men. They quickly dragged Scott into the kitchen. His face was ashen and smeared with smoke, and Lucy saw that the wound on his shoulder was just a graze, but his left leg was bleeding heavily.

"Tourniquet," yelled one of the guardsmen. His face was also sooty and he was bleeding from a head wound.

Lucy immediately pulled off her belt and he quickly wrapped it around Scott's thigh. The other guardsman, whose hands were bloody, was calling for reinforcements. "Shots fired, two men down," she heard him report.

"We have to move back," said Lucy, when a second deafening explosion shook the ground and shattered the windows, knocking her off her feet. "What the . . . ?" she asked.

"Fuel tank," said the guardsman who was tending to Scott.

Cautiously, Lucy crept to the broken window, where she saw the helicopter was now completely engulfed in flames. The heat was intense and she feared the house would also catch fire, but noticed the wind was blowing in the opposite direction, toward the barn. As she watched she noticed a small flatbed trailer containing boxes of the unused fireworks begin to smoke, then burst into flames as it started slowly rolling down the slope to the barn, shooting off rockets and stars that exploded with loud pops. It was stopped at the wall of the silo, sending up a spectacular show of flaming color as fountains, strobes, and flowers ignited. Within seconds the wooden shingles began to smoke and, as she watched, horrified, the entire base of the tall tower was consumed with flames, which quickly rose upward, the silo acting like a chimney. Taylor was trapped, there was only one way down, and it was aflame.

There was a moment when Taylor's head appeared in the window, as she looked out and realized her perilous situation. What would she do? Would she jump? Could she hope to survive such a fall? And what then? She would certainly face shame, a public trial, and years in jail. And what about her family? Would they forgive and support her, or disown her? All those thoughts were flooding Lucy's mind when she heard a single shot and watched horrified as the tower began to crumble and fell in flames to the ground.

"What happened?" It was Lily, standing in the cellar doorway. Seeing Scott, she rushed to his side, falling on her knees and holding his head.

"Taylor?" he asked in a weak voice.

"It's over," said Lucy. "Taylor's gone."

Susan and the boys joined Lucy at the window, watching as the fire spread from the tower and quickly, more quickly than she would have thought possible, spread through the hayloft. It burned steadily, consuming the cedar shingles and revealing the roof trusses, which collapsed onto the floor below. Then flames licked out the windows and around the door; the fire took on a life of its own as the huge orange flames roared and smoke filled the sky. There was no way to fight the fire, although the island men fought to contain it by dampening the earth around the barn with garden hoses. Inevitably, the fire eventually burned out, leaving nothing but a smoldering pile of blackened timbers and a charred stone foundation. It was then that two helicopters hove into sight, circled the farmyard, and flew over the trees to land on the lawn. Moments later, armed and uniformed SWAT team members arrived and took charge.

Ben and Will were ordered to continue hosing down the smoking remains of the barn with water, and Wolf and Brad were set to work spraying the remains of the helicopter with fire extinguishers. The wounded Coast Guardsmen were tended to and airlifted to the trauma center in Portland, along with Scott, who was accompanied by Lily. Susan took charge of the boys, shepherding them back to the mansion, where she promised them peanut butter and jelly sandwiches. Lucy felt relief, and also a terrible sense of sadness, as she waited to learn what came next.

"The Coast Guard radioed the ferry and it's waiting for you, they'll get you out in a Zodiac," said Hopp.

"What about you? Are you staying?" asked Lucy.

"For now," said Hopp, with a shrug. "Later, we'll see. Maybe, maybe not."

"I have to get my things," said Lucy. "They're still in my room in the mansion."

"Go on, I'll have the guardsmen contact the ferry to send the Zodiac."

"Thanks," she said, her voice suddenly thick with emotion. She had an irrational urge to hug him, but instead turned and began hurrying toward the house. She was out of breath when she stepped up on the porch, and she felt shaky all over. That's what happened, she told herself, when the adrenaline began to fade, but she barely made it to the kitchen, where she collapsed on a chair.

"Tea with sugar," said Susan, hopping up and grabbing the kettle. "And how about a peanut butter sandwich?"

"It's good," said Walter, speaking with his mouth full of sandwich.

"I'd be grateful," said Lucy. "I've got to hurry. The ferry's waiting for me."

"It'll wait, don't worry. The schedule's shot to hell, anyway."

Something about the matter-of-fact way Susan spoke, juxtaposing the morning's tragic events with the ferry's abandoned schedule, struck her funny bone and she began to laugh and laugh, wiping tears from her eyes and clutching her stomach. The laughter was contagious and both boys, and even Susan, began to laugh with her.

"I guess it was just the relief," she said, finally getting control of herself. "I've got to get a move on."

She gulped the tea, grabbed the sandwich, and went upstairs, thinking this was the last time she'd climb the staircase. In the hallway she paused in the doorway of Scott and Lily's room, noticing a piece of paper lying on one of the pillows. A note?

It was none of her business, she thought, entering the room. She shouldn't be here in this private space. But after all that she'd been through, she deserved to know. So she crossed the hooked rug with flowers and plucked the note off the crocheted pillow sham. It was simply a folded sheet of notepaper with *Dad* written on it. Opening it, she read the simple message: *Daddy, all I wanted was for you to love me.*

Shaking her head, Lucy replaced the note and left the master bedroom. Going into her room, she quickly threw her clothes into her backpack, hoisted it on her shoulders, and went downstairs to say goodbye to Susan and the boys.

Stepping ashore in Tinker's Cove, Lucy felt as if she'd entered another world, another century. It was noisy in the busy harbor, filled with the sound of trucks beeping as they reversed, honking horns, and the roar of motorcycles zooming up the Sea Street hill. She smelled lobster bait and marine fuel, and all around her there was color and movement. Somewhat stunned by it all, she was relieved to find Bill waiting for her. The ferry captain had called ahead, offering to arrange for an ambulance, but she had declined, deciding that her injuries weren't that serious.

"Welcome, stranger," he said, careful of

her injured arm and giving her a gentle hug. "I think we better get you straight to the emergency room."

"I won't argue with you," agreed Lucy, finding that for once she was only too happy to let her husband take charge of her care.

"How are things at home?" she asked, as they exited the harbor parking lot for the short drive to the cottage hospital.

Bill's answer wasn't reassuring. "Uh, we'll discuss that later, after you're fixed up."

Lucy didn't want to wait, she wanted to know what was going on, but Bill wouldn't say anything more. "One thing at a time," was all he'd say.

After her disturbing experience on the island, Lucy's mind was awhirl with dreadful possibilities. "Okay. Just tell me: Is everyone alive? Did the house burn down?"

Bill chuckled as he turned into the hospital parking lot and pulled up at the ER. "Yes, everyone's alive, and no, the house did not burn down. In you go and I'll park the car."

So Lucy, still fretting about her family and figuring something was going on with either Sara or Zoe, most probably Zoe, got out of the car and went through the automatic doors to the emergency room. By the time she'd given her information and handed over her insurance card, Bill had arrived and they sat together in the unusually empty waiting area. She was about to press him for more information when her name was called and they went together into the exam room.

"So you were attacked by a hawk?" asked the young doctor, sounding skeptical.

"That's right. It happened yesterday. I was on an island and this was the soonest I could get here," explained Lucy.

A nurse carefully unfastened Lucy's sling and unwrapped her bandages, revealing the rather soggy and crumpled basil leaves that Susan had applied to her arm. "My goodness," said the surprised nurse. "What is this?"

"Basil." For a moment, Lucy was back in the kitchen on the island, and Susan was carefully tending her wounds. "There were no antibiotics," she said, returning to the present, "so the woman who took care of me put on the basil; she said it fights infection."

"Well, I guess she was right," said the doctor, studying Lucy's wounds. "There's no sign of infection, and whoever cleaned your wounds did a very good job, but I think we'll get you started on an intravenous antibiotic, anyway." He gave the nurse a nod and specified some drug that Lucy had never heard of, then asked Lucy if she had any other wounds.

"Well, there's my shoulder, and I got a good knock on the head, too," said Lucy.

"All from that hawk?" asked Bill, suspiciously.

Lucy remembered being dragged through the brush by Taylor and fighting desperately for her life by hanging on to that nesting burrow, but all she got out of that encounter was some scratches and sore muscles. "All from the hawk," she said, deciding not to tell Bill about her harrowing brush with death, at least not yet. One thing at a time, wasn't that what he said?

"A tetanus booster, then, and I guess we'd better get an MRI of your head, just to make sure there's no concussion or bleeding," said the doctor. "But it's just a precaution. All in all, I'd say you were pretty lucky."

Lucy met Bill's eyes. "I sure was," she said, smiling.

When they arrived at the house, a couple of hours later, Lucy couldn't help feeling that her luck had run out. She knew something was wrong, but Bill had refused to enlighten her, telling her only that she'd find out soon enough.

Everything looked fine when they pulled

into the driveway; the house was quiet, and there were no shooting flames, gunshots, or exploding fireworks. But when she entered the kitchen she was greeted by Sara with a rather curt, "About time you got home." Then, noticing Lucy's bandages, Sara asked, "And what happened to your arm?"

"A hawk attacked me."

"Really? I never heard of such a thing."

"Me either," said Lucy, turning to greet Zoe, who had emerged from the family room. So this was what Bill had been reluctant to tell her, she realized, taking in Zoe's disheveled state and listless demeanor. "What's going on?" she asked, embracing her daughter and getting an unpleasant whiff of her unwashed body and dirty clothes.

Taking a step back, she noticed her hair was dirty and uncombed, and she hadn't brushed her teeth in some time. Zoe didn't answer her question, but stood mutely, with her head bowed down.

It was Sara who was only too happy to provide the answer. "Mike broke up with her."

"That's terrible," she cooed, in the most sympathetic voice she could muster. Inwardly delighted at the news, she knew she could not share that reaction with her heartbroken daughter. "When did this happen?"

"The day after you left," said Bill, in a somewhat resentful tone that implied she should have been home to deal with Zoe's breakdown.

"Well, sweetheart," she said, taking Zoe by the elbow and leading her to the stairway, intending to get her into the bathroom, "he didn't deserve you, that's for sure, and you'll feel better if you clean yourself up."

Zoe, however, wasn't about to go along with this plan. "I loved him," she declared, dramatically, collapsing onto the kitchen floor in a puddle of grief.

Lucy, Bill, and Sara all shared exasperated glances. Sara rolled her eyes and stomped off, Bill shook his head and threw up his hands in a gesture of helplessness, and Lucy was shocked to discover a surge of anger welling within her. She'd had enough of hysterical young women who wallowed in their emotional cesspools and thoughtlessly destroyed other people's lives. Enough was enough, and that's what she told Zoe.

"You're going to get cleaned up if I have to have your father carry you upstairs and dump you into the bathtub, and don't think I won't," she declared.

Zoe stopped crying and sniffed, giving her

mother a defiant look. Seeing Lucy's expression, she thought better of it and got to her feet. "Okay," she said, shuffling across the kitchen and slowly, very slowly, hauling herself up the stairs. A few minutes later they heard the pipes groaning, a sure sign that she was taking a shower.

Somewhat relieved, Lucy turned to Bill. "What happened? Do you know why they broke up?"

"Yeah, after Zoe moped around for a couple of days I went to see him, to let him know how upset she was and how angry I was that he'd led her on and let her believe he really cared about her."

"What did he say?"

"He denied leading her on, he said he didn't understand why Zoe didn't realize he wasn't that into her, that's how he put it. At first I was furious, but then I thought she really had glamorized him; the guy was really kind of pathetic, and it seemed to me she really had projected her own feelings onto him."

"Yeah," said Lucy, sighing. "I pointed out his many flaws to her, repeatedly, but she refused to see them. It was her first serious relationship and it's a shame she picked such a loser."

"Uh, well, that's the thing, Lucy. He isn't

really a loser at all. She was right about that. It seems he sold this computer game he's been working on for millions of dollars and he's heading out to the west coast to set up his own software firm. It looks like the guy's going to be a billionaire."

"You must be kidding," protested Lucy, sinking onto one of the pressed-wood chairs that surrounded her round, golden oak table.

"No, it's true." He flipped through the pile of newspapers that had accumulated on the table in her absence and, finding the one he was looking for, passed it to her. It was a business section from the *Boston Globe,* and a grinning Mike Snider was pictured under a headline that read: MAINE WHIZ KID HITS JACKPOT WITH GAMBLING VIDEOGAME.

The story went on to detail how Mike had created an algorithm that was widely applicable and would revolutionize software used not only in computer games but in many other computer programs. Mike Snider, the writer concluded, was on line to be the next tech billionaire.

"Just think, if things had gone differently, Zoe could have married a billionaire. Maybe set up a foundation, like Bill and Melinda Gates."

"Or discovered too late that her husband

was very rich, but still a loser," said Lucy, getting a big chuckle from Bill.

"So what do you say to Chinese takeout for dinner?" suggested Bill.

"Perfect," agreed Lucy, thinking it was just one of the many things she'd missed while on the island.

The next morning, confident that she had restored order at home, she had Bill drive her to work. "Are you sure you're ready?" he asked. News of the explosion on the island and Taylor's suicide was just breaking, and they had heard a brief report on the morning TV news and he was beginning to realize that Lucy had been through a more traumatic experience than she had let on. "Don't you want to talk about it?"

"Later," she said, with a sly grin. "First I want to write about it. Believe me, I've got a hell of a story to tell."

ABOUT THE AUTHOR

Leslie Meier is the *New York Times* best-selling author of more than twenty Lucy Stone mysteries and has also written for *Ellery Queen's Mystery Magazine.* She is currently at work on the next Lucy Stone mystery. Readers can visit her website at lesliemeierbooks.com.

The employees of Thorndike Press hope you have enjoyed this Large Print book. All our Thorndike, Wheeler, and Kennebec Large Print titles are designed for easy reading, and all our books are made to last. Other Thorndike Press Large Print books are available at your library, through selected bookstores, or directly from us.

For information about titles, please call:
(800) 223-1244

or visit our website at:
gale.com/thorndike

To share your comments, please write:
Publisher
Thorndike Press
10 Water St., Suite 310
Waterville, ME 04901